CW00455795

Thank You

I wrote this when I severely doubted myself an
in this world. So instead of wallowing I decic
and see where it took me

If you don't like it, that's fine, if the timeline seems *squiffy,* then
that's fine as well. If you think the characters are naff, then that's ok
as well, my mind made them, they aren't going to be offended

If anything, just let this encourage you to pick up a pen (or nowadays
a laptop/computer) and just start writing.

Thank you to: Lisa Gadzikwa and family for her strength. My siblings
Bonnie, Jennifer, Michelle, Christopher and Vincent for. My Mum
and Dad, Janet and Jim Belledonne, for making me via marital
relations and bringing me up right. For my mother-in-law Audrey
Mullin, for showing me what true grit really is and finally Kim and
Leigh, for lending me their brother for a bit.

Disclaimers

ISBN: 978-1-5272-5068-0

Cover Illustration Copyright © 2019 by Kathy Mullin
Cover design by Kathy Mullin
Proof read by Lisa Gadzikwa

Published Independently by Purple Panda Music Management, Liverpool, UK

For Nathaniel, Cecile and Keith

Mirrors

Chapter One – Death

Isabelle Miller (Previously Isabelle Lange) nee.
Domincia 28th April 1982 – died. 5th May 2064

I died on the 5th May 2064, aged eighty-two. It wasn't a notable death, I just kind of *popped* off in my sleep and never woke up. I never had any family around me and a post mortem would later reveal how I had suffered heart failure. My heart simply stopped beating. Regardless, I was still dead, I had lived my life, an interesting life to say the least.

I sometimes wish my death could have been all gun blazing and dramatic, so I would have a more interesting tale to tell, but we don't choose how we go. In any case it is my after-life that has proved more interesting. It was the oddest experience ever, as I left my body and saw my final breath. Even though I was well clear of the vessel, the scientist in me was thinking "ooo that's proof your brain stops before the mechanical functions of the body". I looked myself in the eye, and my body, even without a spirit it managed a smile. For a second it made me think, whether there was little bit of me left in there.

I died with my eyes open, and it was quite hilarious watching my eldest son Nathaniel, attempt to close them when I was in full rigor. They kept popping back open, which in turn made my granddaughter Lucy, cry even more. Nathaniel has never been known for his patience, he simply covered my face with the sheets, then went on to chastise Lucy for being overly sensitive. I don't know where that boy got that insensitivity from, but the girl's grandmother was flat out cold and staring into nothing, she had a right to be a little upset.

As someone who didn't believe in God or any other organised religion, I was quite surprised to be floating round this afterlife. I wish I could send a message to my long-term friend Lisa, finally settling arguments we used to have over a cheeky gin and tonic, answering the question; what happens when we die? As it turns out, we are not just lashed in a ground and worm food, as I once drunkenly described it. I do however maintain my smugness, as no sort of religious being from the Christian faith, or any other religious organisation has approached or guided me as to what the hell I am supposed to be doing.

Well Lisa, if this sees the light of day, I can tell you now, it's all a bit mad, I saw my own funeral, it was a great celebration, and I owe you a massive thank you on getting my wish to have an open casket with all my fabulous make up done so well! I saw you consoling my children, Nathaniel and Bella, and I also saw you sneak the red sauce packets from the buffet into your handbag for later. I haven't met my beautiful husband Karl yet, but I assume that he's either alive and started a new life with a new family, or he passed away a long time ago and he's already reached some higher sense of being. Since his mysterious disappearance, I still hope that instead of the new family theory, he really was kidnapped by aliens in Delemere Forest. *"The Truth is Out There"* as they say.

Another interesting thing about this afterlife malarkey, is that I am not an old lady anymore. My memories are eighty-two years of age, but my body is a lovely thirty-eight, assuming it is my body. I'm not a zombie or anything; stomping round a deserted forest eating dear guts and grunting, I am on the earth, but a completely separate plane of existence to one that the living can't see. I am walking amongst you. I know it's not heaven cos my do-gooder church going neighbour, Tilly, sometimes walks with me. If there was ever a soul deserving of heaven, it was her, and boy was she disappointed that she didn't get to go. However, she still remains hopeful that her omnipresent Lord, who even though he appears to have abandoned her here, that 'He' is going to pull through for her. She might even put in a good word for me. I've told her though I would rather hunt down that beautiful husband of mine in this afterlife, so I can nag him to some kind of second death. She laughed at my naivety, but oh how I have missed him.

I used to believe that after his mysterious disappearance, he that he was by my side when I was living. In some cases, I still believe that, but from his apparent his absence from my afterlife, which would be my version of heaven, I am wondering what's happening as I have all these questions that are meant to be solved by the religious version of death. But they haven't and I want to know why I am just kind of wondering round looking and laughing at things that when alive, are completely unspoken about.

I have entered this death thinking that I am going to be wondering round until I find some sort of conclusion.

Where is my husband? Where are my miscarried babies that I lost when I was in my youth? Also, insignificant questions such as, "do I sleep? Does a 'ghost' dream? Why am I here?

Tilly has filled in some blanks, such as If we don't rest, we become exhausted and that's when we start to show ourselves to the living. Have you ever wondered why ghosts are so angry when they are caught on camera? They are absolutely shattered. I know myself, and even the living version of me; not having enough sleep would make me cranky. There is no secret *'ghost'* code about being caught on the living's camera, and also no express ticket to some sort of fictional Hell if you are caught creeping on some shop's CCTV. However, if it's a place you quite like to visit and you get caught multiple times, all those parapsychologists turn up with their beeping equipment, and the noise of those silly machines can really get on your nerves when you are trying to relax; there has to be some sort of peace in death.

Tilly often visits her old local church and aims to get really tired, this is so she can gracefully walk up the central aisle in her old wedding dress, to terrify her "Church Summer Fayre Bake Off" rival, Meredith Bowker-Smith. It's the small things I suppose, but if it keeps her amused while we find the conclusion to this after-life, it's all good stuff.

It is important to note that showing yourself to the living can be quite a traumatising experience for the living person, they can actually go clinically insane. No one will ever believe that they saw you, and it all ends up with a lobotomy and electric shock treatment which is never good.

I just hope that there is an end, I mean imagine living forever, under a completely different set of metaphysical rules to anyone you love, and your only company being that annoying neighbour who kept posting "Jesus loves you" leaflets through your door when you were alive.

Chapter 2 -Life goes on - for the living and the dead

My grandchildren Lucy and her overbearing 'man-child' husband Joe, have taken over my old house. I use the term 'husband' loosely. He will spend thousands of pounds on computer games and computer equipment for his 'man cave' but won't put a ring on her finger as "it's too expensive". Commitment phobia is not a new phenomenon, and it's been going since I was first married in 2004 to my first husband. Governments tried to bring "being married" back into fashion with really awful and small tax break incentives but it just didn't happen. A whole industry of wedding preparation emerged, but instead of offering lower prices like most supply and demand businesses, they went upwards and extortionate. Still, civil fees were low, it was people's vanity that stopped many people getting wed and Joe was vain.

Anyway, as the only ones in the family without a roof over their heads and a set of twins on the way, their father, my eldest Nathaniel, overruled his sister, Bella, and proceeded to move Lucy and Joe into my old home. I was barely cold before that oaf Joe, destroyed my beautiful vintage wardrobes with some luminous green paint like in one of those stupid decorating programmes. Computer games room indeed, he's a grown man. However, it was through visiting my old home without Tilly as my guide that I discovered the magic of the mirrors.

I was walking round following Joe and Nathaniel as they sorted through my things. I wasn't a hoarder exactly; I just kept a lot of sentimental things. In hindsight, a lot of good that did me; that saying is true, you can't take possessions into the afterlife! Watching them throw out my ticket stubs from concerts that I went to, football matches, including the stubs to the games that I met Bella's father, it left me a little disheartened, oh well I suppose they kept me happy in life.

When they reached my bedroom and there the very pregnant Lucy was sorting through my clothes. I didn't dress like an "old lady" but certainly didn't follow that new-fangled androgynous, multi-coloured mess, that the youth were wearing when I died. When I was alive, I would look at them and the old *Scouse Ma* in me would come out and think "Jesus, did your Mum not tell you that you looked a show before you went out". Or my own mothers favourite saying "get a hairbrush though that tatty head". I was also conscious I never wanted to start wearing clothes from a certain old ladies' department store.

Advancing in age and the fear of growing old had always haunted me right from an early age. We are always stuck in the constant struggle of always having that one person who would say "ah you're still a baby yet" as if to say, "you don't know anything". I had it all my life.

I was also aware that when you are younger time seems to go so slow. In secondary school, those five years seem like an absolute life time, however as you get into your twenties, you hit twenty-five and it's like by accident you sneeze, five years fly past and you are thirty!

Having children as an uncanny way of aging you. As your baby grows up and reaches their miles stones e.g. tenth birthday, secondary school, growth spurts; you forget that

12

you grow with them. You forget that they were once a little baby and you taught them everything they know. The next thing you know your child is the same age as you when you had him, and the realisation kicks in. You are old.

I feared aging, but never feared looking like an old lady, so my clothes were sometimes not very age appropriate, but I used to dress appropriately at weddings and family events. However, my singing and artistic lifestyle let me have a lot of leeway when it came to dressing much younger than I was. In hindsight I should have used more moisturisers, lotions and potions for a frozen wrinkle free face, I just never got around to it.

Lucy was looking at what she wanted to keep clothes wise as apparently 'vintage' never goes out of fashion, vintage?? The cheeky thing never knew I was a full on black haired, black eye make upped Goth back in the day, Nanny doesn't do "vintage" darling. The remnants of my goth days I still wore to the day I died, my precious nose ring.

It was quite comforting to know that my granddaughter had inherited my sentimentality, and separately my love for a blue-eyed man. I knew she sensed my presence, as she had always been a bit sensitive to the spiritual world. The night terrors she kept getting after her grandfather went missing, were the only thing that convinced me and oddly comforted me that he had in fact passed away, rather than he'd have run off with another woman who shared his love for hiking in woodland.

It was during this sort out that I passed by the dressing table mirror and it wasn't myself I saw back. It had turned into what can only be described as a muddy puddle or a grey storm cloud. I looked closer and the centre of the mirror began to clear. It was like looking at a television that sucked you into the experience. A curtain opened and I saw me on the hospital bed in Liverpool in July 2005, giving birth to my Nathaniel. I closed my eyes and then suddenly I was on the bed reliving the entire pain; which can only be described as pooping out a flaming hot bowling ball. Each push re-lived and that annoying midwife repeating "one more push Mrs Lange".

With the fully emerged boy crying his little head off, being taken away to be weighed and tagged, just like a little tiny prisoner. He was passed to me and his father, my first husband Matthew and we spent ages just fawning over this wee tiny lump of human being that I had pushed into the world. Being in my current privileged position of being deceased, I now see that we are prisoners in our own bodies from the day we are born, our bodies limit so much of our imagination and ability to think 'outside the box'.

I blinked again and with a whoosh, there I was suddenly back in the present and in the room where Lucy was weeping over an old Dior cardigan of mine. She was talking with her father and Joe about some sort of false memory that I had worn it to her eighteenth birthday party even though I know I didn't, but it doesn't matter now.

Intrigued by the mirror I went back and the same swirling pattern of mud and clouds was on there. In fact, when I looked at all the mirrors in the room, the hand mirrors, the hall mirrors, I decided to experiment. I went to the hall mirror and said to it "I want to see the birth of Bella". I looked closer and the centre of the mirror cleared where I saw myself, this time in the birthing spa that I went to have my beautiful only girl, Bella and with a blink, I was there.

Bella, is the only child of mine and my beautiful husband Karl. In the courting period I had the honour to be surrounded by the most artistic creative and free loving people I know. We are not talking about the Seventy's hippies who tied themselves to trees, have long hair and wear a LOT of brown clothing; but we are talking about the more modern-day equivalent, you know the type, socialists, musically inclined people.

See in the year 2001, there was the destruction of USA's Twin towers in New York. This led to a catastrophic war, which was later dubbed in history books as the thirty-year war. I'm not going to go all political, however various corruptions in the Middle East, atrocities funded by the western world which lead to this relentless fighting between governments and rebel groups until it later became a massive blur of who the enemy actually was. It was only in 2031 when there was mass immigration from the United States barren lands to the oil rich desert, the conspiracy theorists were proven right. The war was about who controls the worlds power source, oil. The USA colonised the Middle East as the world watched in horror at their undisguised mass genocide of people and in the blood of those women and children and innocent men slain, they started repopulating the areas with the families of the rich American corporations and white picket fence houses containing the "nuclear family". The artistic and friendly creative people I was now surrounded by, these anti-war protestors, were the Bob Dylan's and Joan Baez of the 21st Century and they were truly beautiful people.

Karl was my muse and partner and my husband. He was an intellectual, a musician and most of all he loved football, the English type, not soccer. Everton were our team and we bonded over what can only be described as "man talk" over which players were injured and how well we were going to beat the rival team, Liverpool FC. We both had our flaws and yet we were both middle children and knew the whole "centre of attention" syndrome we both 'suffered' from. We courted then we married on the 3rd June two years after we met and Bella was born twelve months after that.

We were in a position where we could afford a private health suite which was beautiful and not as clinical as when I gave birth to Nathaniel. The midwives were more new age spiritual people, encouraging the "embracement of the inner pain relief" by some sort of aura meditation. Needless to say, that 'Crystal Rose', the spiritual midwife turned 'star child', nearly got her head ripped off for not giving me that gas and air pump quick enough. My baby girl came into the world to the sound of her mother screaming and her Dad in his mother's head lock. I cannot tell a lie, childbirth hurts. Magical awesome experience to some people, but not for me. Bella was named by her father as it means *'beautiful'* in Italian.

My memory was abruptly over, and I closed my eyes and when I opened them was transported to looking at the hall mirror, but with this time Lucy also looking into the mirror staring at something. I was tired and was sure she had caught me. Transportation through the memories is exhausting, I must find Tilly, bunker down and get some rest. I left my old home leaving that useless man child Joe, and my over authoritarian son throwing out old school reports and Nathaniel moaning "Mum never read these properly, if she paid me any attention I might not have gone to jail". If ghosts could roll their eyes, I certainly did at that point. Yes son, it was all my fault you decided as an adult to launder drug money for a dirty broker and do time. Buffoon.

I found Tilly at her old church and I told her all about the mirrors I had found in the house. I wanted to tell her about my experience with the mirrors, but I also wanted her to tell me what they are fully capable of. She was quite stern when she warned me that it tired us dead folk out quickly and that leaves us at risk of being seen. She also told me that she knew of spirits who spent their days at the mirror and slowly age their spiritual soul into something unrecognisable and scary if seen by the living. Tilly was quite clear that the mirror does not show the future and will only show me the things I am ready to see and accept. If the mirror was a personal item when I was living, the more involved in the memory I would be. If it was just a public toilet mirror, then I would be able to view and not get involved. However, the same rules of tiredness applied.

Chapter 3 – Mirror Mirror on the Wall

In true Isabelle fashion, and completely ignoring the advice of Tilly, I ventured back to the house I lived because I wanted to look in the mirror as I had always been a bit of a brat. I had tried looking at the mirrors in the church and it wasn't the same seeing some of my favourite moments in life, my graduation for example, from a window perspective. This was my chance to live again, I didn't want my life to flash before my eyes, and I wanted to re-live it, all the memories good and bad. I had also wanted to see where my husband had gone to all that time ago.

In the old house today, I was met with a scene of Lucy and Joe fighting over who had control over the TV remote. Her bump was getting rather large for only five and a half months, however that's what happens when two babies are snuggling away in your belly.

Ignoring their fickle arguments, I tried to find a mirror as I need to find my husband Karl. I lived in hope that he had maybe ventured to a higher version of an after life, as the only way I can accept his non-appearance in MY after life is that he disappeared and not run off with another woman. The more I watched, the more intrigued I was to see if there was a way to see his memories or go back in time? There must be as I had seen my son and daughter born and that was ages ago. I had gotten rid of a lot of Karl's stuff after I was forced to declare him dead when he was missing for seven years, but there was still a lot of his things hidden in the attic. The attic was the only place my brat child and Joe had not destroyed and emptied. I had to find out what had happened to him as even ghosts need closure.

I stood in the hallway looking at the attic roof hatch. "Okay Isabelle" I thought to myself "How's this going to happen?" I looked down the hall and saw Joe striding in front of me in the corridor, looking to go the bathroom when he suddenly walked right through me. That horrible oaf. It felt odd as he passed through me though, something uneasy about him, something different. I had been walked through a few times in the afterlife, usually by Lucy and it felt serene, pleasant, and genuine, like part of their personality manifested into one feeling. Joe's passing through me, felt uneasy, secretive and unpleasant.

I would deal with him later, I had to find a way to get into that attic, I jumped thinking my ghostly form had levitation powers and to my disappointment, nothing happened. My thirty-eight year old manifestation was a little less nimble than I thought, otherwise I would have clambered on the banister and the top of near doorways to climb through. I was starting to get frustrated; "think," I told myself, I closed my eyes and when I next opened them, I was in the attic.

The boxes were all still there, I don't think they had gotten to seeing what was up here yet. That's not unusual, as even when I first moved in here it took me two years to venture up into the attic. Things look slightly disturbed as the dust looked like it had fingerprints and swipe marks across.

I could see Karl's boxes in the back by the corner where it was still very dark. There were only a few cracks in the shingles in order to get some light. It had suddenly occurred to me that I hadn't yet deal with actually being able to touch anything. I hadn't tried since I had first got to being dead. Karl's belongings were in boxes, not out displayed for me. I was trying to find a small shaving mirror that had belonged to Karl

I saw a flinch in the corner, someone or something hiding looking at me. I shouted "come out of there, whoever you are", "don't be afraid". It would appear that the irony of a ghost saying *do not be afraid,* was not lost on me. A translucent looking figure with an ethereal glow peaked out from behind the box. It was what appeared to be a child, a ghost child, no older than about nine-years old.

She had a face I had seen before but can't pinpoint where. I had had a long life and had seen many faces. She was a lot more translucent than me, she looked like an old soul with a young face. She had big blue eyes and long wavy brown hair. I reached out and asked her "hello, what is your name?" She didn't reply, scurrying back like the little mouse she was. This time I reached out my hand. "Come on lovely, I haven't got all day". She gave a cheeky side smile and sneaked out from round the box like an excited puppy. She started talking like she had fallen right out of that old film *Oliver Twist,* but with a scouse accent and with a mouth like a machine gun, firing all sorts of questions. "Alright lady, are you dead like me then?, ahh you must be. How did you get here? How did you die? What are you doing up here?"

"Calm down little one. Right first, my name is Isabell, yes I'm dead, I don't know how I got here and I died in my sleep. Now what's your name?" She looked at me quite cautiously and sat herself on top of another box. "I'm Katie...I've been here ages waiting for someone to talk to".

After finally calming my new friend down, she explained to me how she had lived in the attic since 2024. She can't remember how she died but she knows that since her passing she had seen her face on milk bottles with a phone number and on missing posters. She had tried to find her living family to tell them that she was okay; however when she got there they had moved somewhere else. She explained how she had found this attic and felt safe here so pretty much stayed here since.

She said that she occasionally came down and caused all sorts of mischief, usually by moving cups and keys and watching residents over the years coming and going. She liked the old lady who lived here before *this lot* as she described them. I had forgotten that the ghost version of me was in her thirties and that she probably didn't recognise the younger version of myself. It was with that revelation now that I recognised her face. When I was alive I had seen her in mirrors looking back at me. Just like I have been looking through looking glasses while in my current deceased state, she too must have been looking at what memories of her short life she had.

In the scurry of meeting my new friend I almost forgot the fact that "she often moved things like cups and keys", a skill I had not yet developed or learned to do. "So, tell me young Kate". "It's Katie" she bluntly interrupted. I tentatively said "So Katie, how is it that you can move things and I can't yet?" Kate explained that she had to be tired in order to do it and when she went on to explain it further, It kind of made sense. They said the mirror tired you out if you spent your day sitting in front of it, it's then you become visible to the land of the living. As your ghostly mistiness solidifies into a something visual, it means you can also move things. In some pseudo-paranormal 'science' you become mass in the physical world and mass can move other mass. Who needs the Large Hadron Collider when you have ghost metaphysical babble?

How does one get tired fast? Ah ha! Tilly's teaching did help now and then, and I quickly asked Katie, "Where's the nearest mirror!!" Katie decided that she would like to show me her story because in her words, "the mirrors will tell it better than I can, plus I reckon the mirror knows more about me than I do myself". We held hands and closed our eyes and when they opened again, we both appeared in Lucy's bathroom. We stood in front of the mirror and looked at the swirling grey pool, trying to figure out how this was going to work with two of us. What's that saying, you can teach an old dog new tricks, or is it can't teach an old dog new tricks, whatever it is I am sticking to the first one, you are never too old to learn. Katie's apparition walked into mine and suddenly I was living in her head and looking through her eyes. I could hear Katie's voice say "don't worry, I will lead the way now"

As one apparition we looked through Lucy's fake shabby chic bathroom mirror into the grey whirlpool and suddenly a picture in it had started to form. We found ourselves outside a terraced house in a rough part of the town. It was definitely local to where we were now in my old house, as I had seen it on my travels. It was a lot older than the last time I saw it. We looked around and a more alive version of Katie, round about the same age as her ghost, was just sitting in the street talking to three other girls and one boy. The friends were talking about international pop star Jake Maynard, some of them professing to "his *epic coolness and how sick he is*". All while her boy mate was calling Katie and the three of them daft by trying to reiterate how this Jake Maynard was '*totally in love with himself*'.

At that moment, I saw a woman walking down the street, she must have been in her mid-thirties, pushing a pram with a baby that looked about six months old. Both handles laden with shopping bags of the local frozen food shop. Katie took one look and ran towards her full pelt while screaming "*Muuuum*". Being the imp that she was, she started rifling through the woman's plastic bags presumably looking for some sort of confectionary or treat. "Well Hello beautiful" her tired looking Mum said, "what are you looking for kiddo, stop it you'll wake up your sister"

Just from that one exchange, you could see this was a relationship of family love and togetherness, but the fact there were no treats, just basic food, you could also see it was a period of hard times. If I remember rightly, 2016 was a time of particular austerity. A time where government stripped the welfare state and the poor and middle earners were left in poverty.

Katie then walked with her Mum to what I assumed was her front door, and I watched her struggle with the pram to get in while the child helped carry the front wheels over the step. We were then transported into the house where inside there were more children, a boy who must have been about thirteen was playing the latest football game on his computer console, and in the kitchen was an older girl about fifteen sitting on the table with an array of nail painting equipment. As the alive version of Katie wandered up the stairs, we saw the action but the muffles of sound were drowned out like it was a conversation happening underwater.

Then very suddenly, we were whooshed from the house back into Lucy's bathroom. I was tired and it would appear that the visit into Katie's past had done its job. But as we arrived back in the present, we had to get out of the bathroom mirror asap, as there stood Lucy, who was running a bath.

We closed our eyes from the bathroom and suddenly Katie and I were back in the attic. Katie declared that now was the time to attempt to open this box, her not knowing that I was wanting to find this small shaving mirror of Karl's. Being the expert Katie went straight to the box that I had directed her to, and she lifted the lid. She gestured for me to come to the box, "it's your turn now". I reached inside the box and my translucent skin reached into the middle of and went straight through the contents. Katie looked at me like I was the class dunce. "No, if you want to move the papers, then you have to want to move them". I stood there thinking to myself, wondering why the child speaks in tongues "what do you mean?" I asked rather frustratingly after dipping my hand in and out of the box a few times. "Concentrate" she gasped. I tried again and this time concentrating on really wanting my hand to pick up the paperwork. I reached in and grabbed the papers and as if by magic I grasped them. I could feel the crumpled sheets of paper between my fingers. After not feeling anything between my fingers for a while, It was bizarre to say the least.

I gently took out the paperwork and there it was, a shaving mirror with one of those extendable arms. It wasn't one of those tacky cheap ones, but was an antique one that Karl had treasured. It was a gift from his Mum when he had turned sixteen and had started growing a wisp of a moustache. It was always intended that it would go inside Karl's coffin with him, however without a body, there was never going to be a funeral or a burial, and now I was dead, how could I trust my selfish son to undertake my Karl's wishes, if his body was ever found.

It took a few attempts to pick it up, more concentration was needed to pick up something like a mirror. Before we even attempted to move it, Katie and I had decided that while we were going for it, and save setting it up each time, we would set it in the unused corner of the attic so that we didn't have go through this effort every time we wanted a glimpse. It took the two of us to lift the mirror out of the box. It was quite eerie watching as our concentration lapses and sometimes our spectral fingers went into the solidness of the mirror. We placed it propped on a book by the slate that was loose in the attic, and once it was placed, Katie with her confidence gave the lose slate a further knock which sent it flying to the pavement outside.

"Shitting HELL!" we heard the oaf Joe shout as while cutting the front garden grass, it apparently nearly brained him. Next time maybe, we giggled together.

We were both excessively tired and as I looked into the mirror and saw what I thought was extra crow's feet on my eyes than what I had seen before. Tilly would go absolutely mental if she knew I was getting up to getting overly tired on purpose, and also the potential of being seen by the living. Although she can talk, her wedding marches in the church are highly hilarious and she does it on purpose! My ghostly self, only new to my spiritual existence, recognised that I needed to listen to my elders. Katie looked at me and said "it's not good you know, you don't look very well, maybe you should wait until tomorrow before you have a go". Bear in mind I was going to listen to my elders from now on, Katie being the oldest spectre out of me and Tilly and her. I decided to bunker down in the attic with Katie until tomorrow. For the first time in forty years, Katie had company and she had a LOT to talk about.

Chapter 4 - Katie Lily Hoyland (b. 28th July 2013 – d. 10th August 2024)

Katie was so eager to tell me all about her family and where she came from, that I let her just ramble on. She was born in Crown Street Hospital on an exceptionally hot day in July and was her Mum and Dad's third child. They called her Katie after her maternal grandmother and Lily as a middle name as it was her Mums favourite flower. She had an older sister, Sarah who was only five years older and an older brother, Callum who was only three years older.

In 2013 she was born into a corrupt government who plunged the country into severe austerity. Foodbanks were plentiful and it wasn't just a "pinch" as the government described, but more like a full on python squeezing every last penny out of the working class.

Katie had always been a clever girl, "you've been here before" was something her Mum would often say. She was very helpful round the house with helping with housework and particularly loved the job of hanging the wet clean washing out on the line. Even though her family were always counting pennies, Katie and her siblings never went hungry, although sometimes, because there were three children to feed, her parents often did. Because Katie's parents always believed knowledge was power and their daughter had a natural need to learn, any rare spare money was put towards maths and English self-study books. Unlike her older siblings, Katie had a logical brain and a thirst for knowledge. Katie was never caught up in games consoles like most kids her age, would often play out in the local field, kicking a football round with her boy mates. Her one bragging rights was she once successfully slide tackled the ball of the schools best football player, Lee Martin, which in turn, made her a hero with the school girls for one day.

As it turned out, Katie hadn't lived far from where I lived with my beautiful Karl and my teenage angst son, Nathaniel and my daughter Bella who was at that awkward teenage phase. Our paths had never crossed as we were in a much more financially comfortable place than Katie's family and as much as I am ashamed to say it now, we were snobs.

Her Mum had not worked for more than yearlong stints in different jobs for a long time. In 2012 she was sacked from her job as a legal secretary when she had told them she was pregnant. Of course this was completely against the law, however it is funny how these legal firms often got away with breaking the law. Since then she had been worked in odd jobs, bar maid, chip shop, and even a graveyard! Katie's Dad was a self-employed gardener so work was either in full bloom in the spring, summer and early autumn months but really scarce over the winter months.

Katie had known our family had existed but only in terms of our big gates and six bedroomed detached house. She and her friends would often tell tales about how certain local celebrities would often turn up to parties at our house, or the mad woman who lived there (me presumably) had often sunbathed naked behind the big walls and that it must be true because her Dad's gardener mates had seen her in the buff one day! For the record, I never sunbathed naked. It's England, there's barely sun and if there was sunbathing there was definitely swimwear present.

Katie was a happy imaginative and bright ten-year-old with her whole future in front of her. Her 'tom boy' personality was what kept her whole family positive in the face of really tough times.

Katie had always insisted that she didn't know how she died and her reaction seemed quite genuine. Obviously from the missing posters her body was never found nor was it discovered by anyone what had really happen to her. My gut was hoping that she wasn't a victim of some sort of paedophile and has been buried as some sick and twisted shame. Regardless of how she died, it was comforting to know that the spiritual realm and whomever it was governed by, had decided that children shouldn't know this information. Katie knew she was running in the dark to collect a forgotten bag from a pub. That was all the information she was willing to offer so I didn't want to push her even more. I hoped and prayed to anyone who would listen, that she wasn't snatched by an opportunist, as most documented murders of this type often occurred. As she had lived as a ghost, she had taught herself how to wander round and eventually how to get to the attic, move things and generally be a little bit mischievous.

She had over the years visited the streets where her family was, but one day they weren't there anymore. Katie was insisting that her Mum had probably forgotten about her by now and she looked a little disheartened at that. My heart sank at the idea that a mother would forget the love for an absent child, so I assured her that I was also a Mum and that am sure her own Mum missed her very much and that there isn't a day she doesn't remember her little girl. She looked a little unconvinced at that but still a little consoled.

So, after talking on for what seemed like an age, about the many years she had been alone as a ghost and all the tales she had to tell about the people she had watched and seen grown old. Also the feelings of sorrow when she talked about how she missed her friends and family. All this talking had tired her out and the little girl fell asleep in the crook of my arm. With that much weight on her shoulders finally shifted, I reckon this would be the most peaceful sleep she had ever had since her death. My own eyes began to get heavy and I too started to drop off. Tomorrow would be a new day.

Chapter 5 - Karl Roger Miller – (b. 7th March 1975 – unknown)

With a sudden banging on the attic door we were startled awake. Was someone coming up to the attic? We needed to hide, only because I am not sure we have recovered enough from our mirror carrying escapade in order to not be seen. We heard a step ladder being set up and someone start to climb with Lucy's muffled voice saying "Please be careful Joe, I can't catch you if you fall, and I really don't think you should be wearing flip flops on a step ladder". As a precaution we hid behind the boxes with Karl's Mirror. From our angle we could still see someone opening the loft hatch, gently at first then the hatch was flung open and we saw the excited eyes of Joe the Oaf. "Lucy babe, this is a massive space and would make a great multimedia room when the babies are born", he shouted back down the hatch. Lucy's exasperated voice shouted "Joe, the babies don't need a multimedia room, they need a nursery". I could sense her eyes rolling at the very suggestion. She's never been good at hiding her true feelings, her face gives it away.

I turned around and Katie had just disappeared, feeling panicked I looked around and couldn't see her but then I looked back to Joe and could see Katie stood right in front of him. She was laughing and shouting "come out, he can't see, look", she blew a raspberry in his face. Feeling a little confident, I came out from the side of the boxes just to check he couldn't see. In true Isabell fashion I managed to bang my backside into some papers resting on another box, making them fall to the ground. "hold on Katie I thought you said I could only move stuff if I concentrated and wanted to". She giggled again, "yeah well sometimes it's just random and out of our control"

With the falling papers Joe jumped. "err babe I'm coming down, it doesn't feel right up here" and Joe went back down the ladder and the hatch was closed. With that nuisance out the way it was time to look at Karl's mirror.

Katie pipped up "you should really do this by yourself, it's really none of my business, anyway I fancy a bit of winding that loft hatch idiot up". I wasn't this little girl's mother and didn't have any authority over her at all, despite how scared I was feeling about seeing through Karl's looking glass, I had to do this on my own. As I was about to answer her that I was okay with it but didn't get the chance as when I turned around, she suddenly wasn't there anymore and. I walked towards his mirror and looked at the muddy puddle that was in there.

I was transported to Karl's world. I saw my husband at sixteen years of age getting the gift of this mirror from his Mum. I could tell it was him, as the young boy in front of me had the same piercing blue eyes my Karl had on the day he went out the door for the last time. I could not believe he looked so much like his Mum and from this exchange I could see that there was that strong mother/son bond.

It was like we were fast forwarded to a time that he was a guitarist in a band. He had a silly hat on and had his guitar so high up (much higher up than I ever saw him wear it) that it could have been a necklace, It was lovely to see my Karl, so talented and obviously enjoying life.

The scene fast forwarded again and I saw him at an Everton football match, the promotional marketing pictures on the side of the ground were the same ones as when I used to go to the match. I saw him look across and see a younger version of myself, and Karl striding across the fan filled 'fan zone' area and "accidently" shouldered me. "Oi" a very brash version of myself said back "no excuse me or nothing...... tosser". The vision then went forward through the match and to the pub after it and I could see how he had spotted me again in the pub after the game. I was laughing and joking with my friends, such the lady drinking a pint of lager. As I lifted the pint glass to my lips and started to drink, our eyes met again. Feeling brave and slightly fuelled by beer and the match buzz, I went up him and shouted through the commotion, "I think you owe me a pint after hurting my shoulder before". The rest, is as they say, history. We were like a whirlwind with countless numbers of dates and gigs, we were unstoppable.

We had such wonderful times together, not to mention a fair few disagreements. I could spend hours looking through his mirror and describing all the great times and stories from our courtship. The funniest times usually involving going on spontaneous days out to some sort of castle or nature walk. One time I had dragged my chain smoking wine guzzling unhealthy man up the hill/mini mountain Moel Famau in North Wales. I have got to give it to him, he did it even despite the diva moaning about it. "If I get tired and you keep having a go, I am just going to go back down" he snapped on that initial steep climb. He was forever the diva but that was part of his charm. He always had a bit of a strop when dealing with something new, then once he had done it, an even crazier idea will spout from his brain.

What was great about him is that he accepted me and my son into his life. I had said to Karl in the first week of us deciding we were officially "a couple" that I came as a pair. If he doesn't want the responsibility of being s step-father (as Nathaniel already had an active father) then he should go now and we can carry on with our lives separately. It wasn't so much the responsibility of being a "step-father" that concerned me, it was more that Karl had to realise my children came first, and if there was a choice between a school play and an important event with him, then I would choose the school play. Karl was fine with this and as we grew up, he recognised that biologically, Nathaniel wasn't his but he always treated him like he was his own, however, carefully toeing the line between his own and Nathaniel's actual father's responsibilities.

As our relationship grew, I had gone on to marry Karl in a humble registry office, and I saw his perspective of my own wedding and I saw a tear fell down his face as he watched his bride be brought to him. What a day that was. Needless to say, there were very sore heads the next day after a live music performance of some of Liverpool's best bands, who gave us the gift of their music, rather than of chintzy pottery.

As a band wife I often found myself in situations that a girl from a working class background had never encountered. Back stage at gigs wasn't the exciting party you thought it was, in fact it was rather boring listening to people catch up, who despite acting inseparable on stage only saw each other on the actual night of the gig. Depending on whose gig it was and who the support acts were, depended on the level of conversation. With the Socialist type bands the conversations were always political high risers. With the more earthy type bands it was always a bit existential vegan clap trap. The younger bands were all so very "rock and roll", often chatting absolute bubbles over how they have recorded three singles, making it pretty big, but had to go home early as their job in a coffee shop was an early shift. Being the girl from the run-down estate, and was a bit 'too' common sense and cynical, I didn't care how important a person thought they were, they got the real me, no sycophancy, and if you were a bit of an idiot, I wouldn't engage with them. As it was Karl's mirror it often went to him talking to other people, while I was swanning round in the background, him saying to other people "she's mad but she's mine".

Stepping out of his mirror for a second, despite the nostalgia of the events I had seen, I thought that it was interesting that I could hear conversations that there was no way I could have heard at the time in the living world. This must mean they weren't in my head and that the personal nature of this mirror meant part of Karl's memories were 'stored, if that's the right word, in the glass itself.

When I looked back into the mirror, I found myself immersed in memories. I was enjoying seeing how he had introduced me back into singing and let me find my voice again. Also, how we formed our cabaret duo as a side project of his regular band thing so we could build a life together. Even heavily pregnant with Bella I was singing *"Etta James's At Last"* in the same play list as heavy rock and alternative indie tunes at mad gigs and social clubs around the country. When we eventually formed a bigger band by adding our saxophone player, Edward, our drummer, Lauren, it was growing into a whole new beast. I learned bass guitar and the whole experience and time was just an amazing evolution of sound. It was this business that let us buy our first big house, the one that eventually Katie and her friends had told stories to each other about.

As I watched and to my utter shame, I see how I had failed to notice my teenage son start with his moods and arguments with Karl. Its only now through this mirror do I see the arguments they had which nine times out of ten started over something simple like a coat being left on the floor, ended with "you're not my Dad" and finally to Karl and him shouting "well go live with him then". All standard teenage angst stuff, well at least I thought it was standard, I clearly took that for granted.

Regardless of his tantrums, Nathaniel had passed his GCSE's with flying colours and went on to do his A Levels. He always had a natural ability to learn and was scarily intelligent, and this was in spite his clear contempt of the education system we had put him in. He went into a business and maths A level programme. His lecturers has noticed his natural aptitude and figured his "acting out" was an indication that his A Levels were not challenging enough for him, as during his second year in A Levels he was invited by a local university to complete a foundation degree after being recommended by the same college lecturers.

This was about the time his attitude completely changed, he was getting too cocky. In my 'mother's pride' of his amazing grades and achievements I never saw his sheer arrogance develop and in retrospect, I was now seeing it happen in the antique shaving mirror on how he made his step father and his little half -sister's life a living hell while he tried to establish himself as "King of the Castle". Nathaniel made a point of calling Bella is half-sister, in a tone that sounded like he was spitting the words out. He did this as a way to torment her and exclude her and her Dad from anything called "family". It was like he utterly resented mine and his father's divorce and in turn blamed Karl and Bella for that.

Karl, despite this resistance from Nathaniel, had tried his best to keep the peace and his mirror was showing this. While watching I couldn't help but get upset and have this utter feeling of regret that I didn't try harder to keep the peace, or even notice it in the first instance. I wish I could find him now to tell him that it was my fault.

Chapter 6 - Back to Reality as we know it

"ISABELLE"

It was Katie shouting at me, my eyes opened and I was back in the attic. "You were crying" she said, "don't cry, you can't change the past, we can only make it right". Katie was reassuring me as best as she could but I think it all got a little too much. With these young lady's old and wise words, I think I found this was my reason that I didn't go to my "Other place" after death. I am pretty sure that I couldn't rest in peace as I had to find my husband, not just for my selfish needs to have afterlife companionship, but to let him find his afterlife and tell him that it wasn't his fault.

Katie wiped my tears, but then went on to tell me how she had been running around the main house knocking all sorts of cups and ornaments onto the floor whenever the Oaf walked past. She had decided that she could only push him so far, but she was satisfied that he was adequately freaked out when she sat next to him in the garden throwing pebbles into the pond, and when he went to investigate the random plops, Katie then started throwing the pebbles at him. He really got freaked out and started to run in to Lucy like a frightened puppy. Katie had decided that she quite likes Lucy, so she had decided to give the Oaf a break.

I thought that I must let Tilly meet my new little friend, as they seem so alike, with Tilly's dalliance for a spot of mischief with her wedding dress runs, I think they would share a sense of humour that would make them get along. I had asked Katie whether she had wanted to visit my place where I stay and meet my friend, and she was quite agreeable to this. "Yes, more friends" she said quite excitedly as she skipped towards the attic hatch. Travelling to the church, I realised that this time I would have to be more careful. This was because I had been staring in the shaving mirror for some time, and may be slightly visible. So, after carefully navigating out of the house, Katie and I headed towards the old church to find Tilly.

The walk was really quite enjoyable with my little companion, and I discovered lots about her personality, mainly her ability to talk. After having my ear bent off by Katie on the walk there, we got to the church quite late. This is how I found out that apparently time flies when you're dead, who knew! This must be why whenever ghosts are caught on camera in all those mad shows, they always seem to be moving at a slower speed. It's more like they are normal speed but the living world is too fast. Paradoxes within conundrums, too much thinking for someone who no longer has a living brain.

When we got to the church we were greeted by a very worried and slightly agitated Tilly. "Where HAVE you been?!?" she was apparently beside herself with worry enough to shout at us at the top of her lungs. I really don't know what the shouting or worrying was for, it's not like I could die again (could I?). "Calm Down dear", I said in my best Michael Winner impression, and if looks could kill, I would be dead again, she wasn't impressed. By this point, Katie had hidden behind my legs, which is little bit pointless when you are transparent though.

"So Tilly, this is my friend Katie, she lives in my old house in the attic", I gently introduced my new little friend. Tilly soon changed that frown, firstly into a confused look, and then a big smile when her eyes connected with Katie's. Tilly was cautious in her introductions, and so as not to scare her she held out her hand and gently said "well Hello Katie, its lovely to meet you". Tilly was interested in Katie's story, so after I had let her know about our adventure into Katie's mirror and her story so far, Tilly wanted to get into specifics about how Katie died and whether we could as a group help figure it out.

The Death of Katie Lilly Hoyland.

After all the introductions and the stern telling off from Tilly, we went and sat in our place of hiding, where we would normally go to rest. Tilly had such a way in getting the little visitor to speak openly, something that my blunt "out with it" attitude wasn't good with. Tilly managed to coax Katie into telling us more about her very short life.

Katie told us how she was the only one out of her siblings who ever helped their Mum out around the house. The new baby, Daisy, whom she only knew for six months, when Katie had passed away. She told us how her Mum fainted when she found out she was having a baby. Little Katie was stood outside the bathroom door when her Mum took a special test, and she remembers all her Mum kept uttering was "there's no chance, not a chance". Katie remembers the pregnancy developing and her Mum's bump getting bigger. The bigger the bump got, the more she would have to help, so she helped her mum with jobs.

Jobs such as helping her Mum tie her shoe laces as her massive bump got in the way and she couldn't tie her laces on her trainers on her own. As well as being her Mum's 'executive shoe lacer upper' Katie did a lot of the work in helping her get dressed. Katie even remembered the day the new baby was born and even remembers being there when her Mum *'wet her pants, cos the baby was fed up living in her tummy'*. The panic that her Dad was in when it happened made her giggle as well, but remembers being upset at not being able to be there with her Mum in hospital and crying as her Dad took her, Sarah and Callum to their Nan's in Wavertree so their Mum could go to the Maternity hospital.

After going to school the next day and coming home, the three Hoyland kids were taken to the hospital to meet little Daisy-May Hoyland. Despite the excitement of having a new baby in the house, things were weird, Katie told us her Mum was asleep with her back to her children in the bed while the new baby wiggled in the Perspex hospital cot. When Katie had asked what was wrong, her Dad explained that Mum had a difficult time and had spent a long time trying to get the baby out. The midwife who had come in the room to take measurements while the visit was happening chirped in "older Mums usually take longer, don't worry". Her Dad had asked the midwife to leave, he was clearly annoyed with that mindless comment from the midwife. Katie's Mum had started crying, still with her back to her visiting family. Regardless of all this commotion, Katie said she remembered looking into the cot and baby Daisy was little and squishy and amazing.

When her Mum and the baby finally came home, her Mum had managed to find her spark again. She was confident again and able to deal with a busy household and make it look completely effortless. Katie was completely obsessed with the new baby and always followed her Mum around, which meant she also became her Mum's confident. Katie was probably too young to hear some of the problems she was hearing, but at the same time she had felt honoured that her Mum was sharing with her. "Normally Sarah was Mum's favourite" Katie exclaimed "but she had turned into a smelly teenager and only bothered with Mum when she wanted money". Katie continued to tell us how she helped her Mum with all sorts of baby related things, bathing, nappy changing (even the poo nappies). She would see her Mum cry now and then and would hug her to which her Mum said "go away silly I will be fine".

She also heard her Mum and Dad arguing, it was never anything major she had insisted, as if defending her parents' marriage. Most of it was her Dad moaning about how she shouldn't be talking to Katie like an adult. Katie heard it all but never let it phase her. She would still be there for her Mum. They soon made up after the arguments by taking turns looking after Daisy and Katie got sent out to play.

She told us the day she died that it had been a Sunday. She only knew it was a Sunday as it was baby Daisy's christening in the day time. Katie was from a big Catholic family, although none of them had been to church in a good while.

From my own experience of singing in Catholic social clubs, the church wasn't the main feature of modern-day Catholic christenings; instead it was about the family gathering and the party afterwards. I was surprised at the level of detail that Katie could recall from the actual day but still she did not know how she died. I was again thankful that the trauma of how she potentially died was hidden from her after-life psyche.

She remembers that Daisy's christening gown was a hand me down passed from her, and before her it had belonged to her older sister, Sarah. On the actual day of the christening Katie was wearing a dress that had been found at the bottom of Sarah's wardrobe. As was quite normal for the times, if it was too small for the eldest sister, it was just the right size for the younger sister. Her Mum and Dad had got a quick high interest loan off the internet so they could pay for the buffet and the hall hire, and it was a fun day. Katie was up to her usual cheeky forgivable mischief and kept stealing chicken nuggets and cherry tomatoes before the buffet was even opened.

The day was one of celebration and fun. The children were being entertained by a man dressed in a shabby costume of a popular cartoon character. This meant the children were happy, which in turn meant the parents were able to talk and drink. Even Katie's Mum was relaxed and had wine on her table. Her Dad had a few too many too drink, which was to the amusement of Katie who couldn't stop laughing at his tipsy talk. It was about 7pm when her family and the party got kicked out of the pub's function room to make way for the regular Sunday night bingo. There were no kids allowed after 7pm, although there were the chancers who attempted to hide their children in an out of sight corner, they were soon caught and parents politely informed they had to leave. The family all walked home as it wasn't far, while other revellers without children moved to the main lounge to carry on their night drinking. Katie remembers this part as her Nan was one of the ones who went to the lounge and she had to run in without being seen and say goodbye to her.

Katie elaborated and told us that when she got home, her Dad fell asleep on the couch and her sister had gone out with her friends. Callum was hiding in his room away from his mother's wrath. He had gotten grounded at the christening when he had been caught drinking cider, which he had cunningly disguised in a cola can. Her Mum, being the chief steward, disciplinarian and organiser of the Hoyland family went about settling the house down after an exciting day. It was about 9pm when Daisy had decided to fill her nappy up to the point of exploding out the back of her baby grow. Katie went on to say how her Mum had been trying her best to clean Daisy up, but when she went to grab a nappy, she had noticed that the nappy bag wasn't attached to the pram anymore and it must have been left in the club. Her Mum had not wanted to leave the baby covered in her own faeces but needed that bag as, even though she had nappies in the house, the bag had the baby's teething ring in it as well as the baby's eczema cream. Katie was sent back to the club down the road to collect the bag.

Katie had set off out the back door of the house. She ran down the back alley across the park to get to the club. There was only one road to cross and it had a pelican crossing on it. She said she remembered pressing the button and waiting for the green man, and even remembers crossing the road once the green man appeared when it made that siren beeping like noise. Once she crossed the road, she continued to run down towards the pub and when she was at the social club door, she walked in. Once in the place she walked towards the bar and tried to get the attention of the busy lady working behind the bar. Katie kept waving a gesticulating like made, but the lady still didn't see her so she gave up when she failed to get her attention.

So, she went over to the place where she had said good bye to her Nan. It would have just been typical for her Nan to take a bag thinking she was being helpful. Her Nan was no longer there so must have gone but she saw the bag hidden under a chair so and she ran over. It was only when she tried to grab the handle and her hand went right through it, did she realise that there was something wrong.

Katie had started crying. Tilly and I reassured her and cuddled her little weeping form but told her that if she didn't want to continue to tell the story that she should stop now. But curiosity had got a hold of Tilly and she needed to ask her one more question, "Katie, what was your Mum's name?" Katie wiped her tear and said "her name is Melissa". It was at that point we cuddled into her and she fell asleep on us.

We started to ponder, what a sad ending to a happy but short life that our new little friend had had. Together Tilly and I had decided that we needed to find out what happened to her for the sake of this little girl and her family. I hoped that her mother was alive today so I could see what efforts were made to try and bring answers to her daughter's death. I could try looking in a phone book with my newly acquired moving skills, however the last time I saw a phone book was 2026 and am not even sure they exist anymore. This was going to be some considerable effort but it was something that needed to be done. From Katie's first flash back I knew where she lived and our search for answers should start there. However, it was getting late and this would have to wait until tomorrow. We had already risked being seen once today already, by walking across town after having a tiresome look in Karl's mirror. So, with more rest tonight, tomorrow we go for it.

Chapter 7- Melissa Hoyland - b. 17th April 1990- ?

The next morning, I left Katie in the care of Tilly as I wandered the street to try and find where Katie used to live. If I remembered rightly, it was not far from my old house, so that's where I would be headed first, then go from there. I had worked out that her Mum would be younger than me by eight years so hopefully she's still alive today. Thinking back to my little friend's conversations, Katie had said she had been back to her old house only a year after she had died, only to find her family had moved away. I could see why her family would want to move away after a tragedy of losing a child, with the surroundings constantly reminding them of what they had lost. However, I wanted to make sure that they had moved away, because it may be the case that she may have just gone there and they had gone out.

Having being a regular visitor to my old house, it didn't take me long to get there, and then from that point I retraced the steps on where to go from Katie's memory. It took a bit of time, but I eventually found where she had lived. I took a moment to just stand there and look, I'm feeling pretty sure that this was her home, still there after all this time. As I passed through the front door I wanted to see if there was any clues as to what was going on now. I could see from the furniture and house items that this house was definitely still lived in. In the kitchen there was a Formica table, small under cabinet fridge and freezer, a single cooker, and a kettle that looked like it had recently boiled. In the living room there was a large sofa and a chair right up by the window looking outwards. The back door was open and as I made my way outside I could see there was a really old woman sitting in a chair just reading a newspaper. I say *really old* flippantly, I mean, I was eighty-two when my heart decided to stop beating for no reason, but I had always considered myself quite spritely for my age, not as 'old'.

This face in front of me was the face of an *"old"* old woman. She looked completely worn out and disappointed in her life and a little older and frailer than her actual years.

After seeing her name on a doctor's letter on the fridge with a magnet keeping it in place, Melissa Hoyland was her name. Melissa Hoyland was very skinny and petite and wore a pinafore with a cotton dress underneath, support tights and a pair of steady slippers with a faux fur liner. As she potted around making herself a sandwich I decided to take a look upstairs. When I got to the top landing I could see three bedrooms, all of them decorated in a pastel purple colour. I had known from my old houses and from visiting others that pastel purple was the universal colour that indicated "spare room". Two of the rooms had a single bed in them and nothing that made them look like they belong to anyone, however the third bedroom was more telling.

In this room there were pictures everywhere of not just her little girl Katie, but what looks like a great big extended family. Children, Grandchildren and even what looks like a couple of great grandchildren. All the different faces had the similar features, the brown almond shaped eyes, the bump on their nose. In a frame by the bed, there was a picture of a younger Melissa with her husband, Katie and the other children at the christening of the little baby. It dawned on me that this must have been the last ever photo of Katie. Bless her little heart, she will be forever young. They were all smiling on this photo and it upset me that they weren't to know the tragedy that would follow that night?

On the nightstand, there was an open box with newspaper clippings all detailing her daughter's disappearance. The stock photograph they used of Katie's face, was taken from the christening picture. Moving the top papers with my new movement skills, I could see the clippings were from the first couple of days and weeks of her disappearance. As the bottom of the pile revealed themselves, it only featured each year either on the anniversary of her disappearance or her birthday. There was the occasional print out of comment feeds from social media sites where vicious faceless 'trolls' said comments such as, *"parents sending a nine-year-old out that late at night"* and *"ahh well, sure she lost one, she's got three to spare"*. Luckily these comments were far and few between the comments from kind well-wishers and people with genuine sympathy

There were pictures of Melissa with headlines such as, "Mum's grief made her start charity to fund missing person cases". The clippings of the positive stories in the papers of the good work the charity did. However, tragedy was just around the corner as I turned the page, I saw a clipping of her husband, not much older than thirty-five years old, with the headline "Tragic Dad of missing child Katie Hoyland, Travis Hoyland dies of overdose". A tear dropped from my eye as I wondered what has this woman put up with? I am absolutely devastated for her.

I went back downstairs to see the woman, Melissa. This was a woman's whose heart had been broken and shattered, a woman who, if I was alive, I couldn't say "I know how you feel" as I hadn't lost a child.

I wandered into the back garden and sat in a chair next to her where she was nibbling at the sandwich she had just made herself. I could see the same eyes as the lady in Katie's mirror, but they were sadder. A face that has a lot more sagging and wrinkles on, even at only seventy four years of age, She could have passed as ninety if not a day. She was just sipping her tea between bites of her sandwich and looking at the sky. I don't think I was going to learn about Katie's disappearance here, other than the sorrow that her daughters passing left and the face of a woman who had lost it all but kept on living.

As the doorbell went, her head turned. She put down her cup of tea and shouted "Come in, doors open". Obviously she was confident enough that she lived in an area that she trusted not to be burgled by doorstep opportunists. A woman came into the house who must've been in her mid-fifties, followed closely behind her was another young woman in her early twenties'. "Hello Mum" said the older one and the younger one chirped after "Nanny Lis, are you up". Bit late for asking that question I thought, if she wasn't up then she would not have shouted come in!

They came into the garden to see the sad old lady I had just been sitting next to, and with a little more enthusiasm in her voice Melissa said *"hello Sarah dear, hello Kate"*.

It all clicked in my head, this was her daughter and with the younger lady having a look of Sarah, I am going to hazard a guess that Kate was Sarah's daughter. After exchanging pleasantries with her grandma, Kate's head was buried in her phone, texting and playing on her social media accounts with only the whistle of a bird sound, indicating an incoming message reverberating every three seconds

Sarah glanced at her daughter, "can you please put that thing on silent or something, the incessant sound is driving me mad". Switching her gaze back to her mum, Sarah spoke, "Listen Mum" she said, which I thought was quite blunt and harsh the way she spoke to her Mum. Sarah continued, "You know its forty years since Katie's disappeared, and the charity were wondering whether we should do an event or something and a big drive for any information, not just on Katie, but on all the missing kids needed to be found". Melissa rolled her eyes and took another bite out of her sandwich, and Sarah continued to prattle on, "The person who has her could still be alive Mum. She could still be alive and have amnesia". Well that shocked me that after Sarah's initial bluntness to her Mum that Sarah still truly believed her sister was alive. It was an utter shame I knew different and couldn't say anything to them.

Melissa scowled at her daughter, "your sister is dead, I will have no more spoken about it". That shocked me a bit more that after seeing all the clippings and the pictures she kept in her bedroom, that she truly thought that her daughter was dead. Melissa Hoyland may be convincing her kids she didn't care anymore but she certainly wasn't fooling me. Kate took her eyes off her phone then looked at Sarah. Kate rolled her eyes and went straight back to texting/social media posting. After a moment of awkward silence Sarah nudged Kate and she gave an almost silent 'tut' and looked up again. "Annnnnnnnyway, Nan, I am twenty-one   next month, Mum has organised a meal with you all before I go to Ibiza with my friends, do you fancy anywhere special". Melissa broke her hard stance and scowl and said in a soft tone, "no dear whatever you want, as long as it isn't anything spicy".

I left them to their conversations, Sarah and Kate working hard to breakdown their elder matriarch's emotional defence system and after listening there was definitely not much I could learn here. I didn't know whether to tell Katie that her Mum was still alive and in the same house and that her family were still holding out hope she was alive.

Chapter 8 - Nathaniel Michael Lange 5th July 2004 - Present

On the way back to the church, I had decided to go back to my old house where Lucy and Joe were now living, just to see what shenanigans they were getting up to now. As I approached I could see her massive bump as she sat on a sun lounger in the front garden. She may be relaxed yet a little bit uncomfortable now but two babies at the same time, well that is going to be a shock to the system.

Her Dad, Nathaniel, was sat by her wearing his work suit and as I got close, I saw he had a bottle of beer next to him. Strange that he would be drinking midway through the day but oh well none of my business. Forgetting Nathaniel's bad drinking habits for a minute, I decided to have a listen to what they were talking about. It would appear that Lucy was planning a trip to Delemere Forrest in the camper van before the babies were born. Lucy had been that forest with her grandad on countless occasions. It's strange that she remembers those trips, as she was so little when Karl went missing, but old enough to remember him, and now she was trying to explain to her Dad how she wanted to try and connect to her granddad Karl, and tell him all about the babies. She was only five when he went missing in 2049, but those five years she was "Granddad's little princess"

Nathaniel, being the sceptical one squinted his eyes, and with a scowl and said "what's with this hippy dippy bull crap, he's not even your proper Granddad". I wasn't enjoying this side to my son. It would appear he was always good at hiding his nasty streak around me, but when I wasn't watching he was a complete piece of work.

I was in awe at such a vicious boy I had brought up. Lucy looked hurt at his belittling and patronising remark which in turn upset me, as Nathaniel knew as well as me that Karl and Lucy were almost inseparable. He didn't seem to mind me and Karl babysitting baby Lucy so him and his daft dolly bird wife could go and get drunk every weekend.

Nathaniel's own biological father was also shocked at the way his son had turned out. Nathaniel decided to stick him in some cheap nursing home, convincing doctors that he had "lost his marbles" when in fact his mind was still sharper than a knife. Mine and Nathaniel's father's divorce was quite amicable and contact with our son was never an issue. Nathaniel saw his Dad as equally as he saw me, and when he was younger, he loved Karl and loved our days out and time together as a "blended family". It was in Nathaniel's teenage years that this friction with Karl, and any sort of male authority, developed. When Nathaniel went to prison in his late thirties, even then he had a smarmy plan to try and evade authority as he thought that by getting his wife pregnant, the expectant father would have more lenience with the Judge. Lucy was never to know that she was the result of her father's self-preservation plan, but either way she was a blessing and she became one of my and Karl's closest grandchildren.

Nathaniel seemed unnecessarily irate that she wanted to go to Delcmere, "what's the point of even going, he's dead and am pretty sure your real Granddad, wants to see you about the babies. After all, he's still alive and I pay good money for that care home".

Lucy was at breaking point and snapped at Nathaniel, "Please shut up, Grandad Karl is still technically missing, not dead, I visited Grandad Matt only two weeks ago, so you should visit your own Dad more often yourself" Lucy retorted, knowing quite well her Dad hasn't visited his own father for the past six months. She got her sharp tongue and ability for a quick retort from me, that's my girl.

After being placed in that nursing home, the boredom and mundanity of it started to take a toll on my ex-husband and after ten years in the nursing home, Matthew's one sharp mind was now in the throes of dementia. At least he was in the right place with medical experts on hand at all times, if it was left to his son, Matthew would be dead. Matthew's second wife was still alive and still sharp as a tack, but of course she would be, as she was much younger than Matthew by a good eleven years when they married. I only know her name from the fact Nathaniel hated her and whenever he would say her name, "Sophie", in such a venomous way, almost spitting whenever referring to her. She was enjoying her living inheritance from her dementia ridden husband while she still had it, such a powerful tool that "Power of Attorney" legal document was. She often enjoyed coach holidays to Genoa and Lake Como, also every Monday and Wednesday she loved meeting her girls at bingo at the local social club. I had never ever bothered her and she had never bothered me.

Sophie had brought her own two kids to the marriage and never had any more to do with Nathaniel, after a row over putting him in the nursing home. You can just imagine the utter contempt that Nathaniel has for his half-sister and imagine how he felt towards supposed step-siblings that shared not one drop of blood. He was a vicious little thing, I do wonder where this hatred arose from

I used to think Nathaniel had just hated Sophie for the fact she was spending his inheritance, which I secretly thought was an amazing thing. I wish I knew when I was going to die otherwise I would have gone to a plastic surgeon, had everything pinched back, fat sucked out, extra lumps put in, just so it was all spent before he got his grubby mitts on it.

There was suddenly a crash from the back garden, Nathaniel and Lucy ran, and I followed. To everyone's surprise they saw Joe the Oaf, on top of the flat roof of the outhouse/shed with his top half sticking out the top and his bottom half dangling inside. Lucy started fretting "what are you doing?" she was screaming, then I'm assuming it is her heightened emotional state, she burst into tears. Nathaniel hugged his daughter and shouted "what the bloody hell are you doing to my mother's aviary????"

As it transpired, Joe's thought process was that since his supernatural experience in the attic, he had decided a better computer games room would be the old aviary that I had previously kept my cockatiels in years ago, and was now a storage shed. Because of the electrical nature of a potential computer room, Joe needed to test for leaks in the roof; this was without actually going inside the shed in the first place to see if there were adequate support beams inside. He just got a ladder, went straight on to the roof and did not notice the bowing weak spot and he went right through.

Chapter 9 - Karl's Mirror

After the drama in the garden had unfolded, I went back up the stairs to the attic as I thought whilst I was here, I may as well have a glance in Karl's mirror. I climbed the stairs and when underneath the attic hatch I closed my eyes and when I opened them I was in the attic. I went round to our secret corner where Katie and I had previously set the mirror up. It was already quite active swirling away when I looked into it. I knew what I wanted to see this time and I wondered if the mirror knew that my intention this time was to try and find out his last movements before he went missing from my life. I was not sure that the mirror was in for taking orders from me yet, as it appeared to have other ideas. I found myself entered into the memory, this time however, as an observer where Karl was much younger, and around the time he went missing.

The disobedient mirror took me to a night in mine and Karl's home. I walked through the living room to see Karl was in the conservatory trying out some new riffs on his guitar. I don't know where the living version of me was, I must have been out somewhere. I looked on the table and there was a newspaper, still looking untouched with what I had assumed was today's date on it. From newspaper clue and the fact I knew that I gigged most Sunday Evenings, it pointed to the fact it was a Sunday. During my days with Karl, I regularly threw all my papers as soon as they were read, as there weren't many papers who did print editions anymore. I also recycled like a mad woman, so I knew I wouldn't leave an old paper lying round.

I walked right up to my beautiful Karl and sat down next to him and sighed loudly. I knew he couldn't see me but I still put my face right up to his and longed to kiss his lips. I missed him so much. With my sigh he suddenly stopped playing and looked up, for a moment I wondered if he sensed me. He went back down to playing his guitar. He was practicing some new riffs and had been writing new songs. Usually he would be with me gigging on a Sunday night, but I wonder if he was ill or something this night. There weren't many gigs of mine he missed so it was unusual that he was actually home that night.

He continued plucking his guitar and writing down interesting combinations, but this peace was disturbed with a persistent and urgent banging on the back door and shouting. Karl went to the door quickly and it was a younger version of Nathaniel. He must have been about nineteen or so and from the look of him he was clearly drunk and all dishevelled. He entered the house in a state of panic. "Is Mum here?" he said quietly as he barged past Karl. When he saw no sign of me he shouted louder at a bemused Karl, "KARL, FOR FUCKING HELLS SAKE IS MUM HERE!" Karl was clearly taken aback by the panic, tried to grab Nathaniel by the shoulders. "What's happening, what's wrong?" Karl was panicking himself now wondering what had happened. Nathaniel started talking and mumbling, first incoherently then he started to make a little more sense. "I've fucked up, I've fucked up, I can't believe it, I've fucked up". Karl still none the wiser was trying to calm down Nathaniel. "You're drunk, come on kiddo calm down". Nathaniel just looked a Karl with a look of utter distain "don't call me *kiddo*'. He wiped tears from his eyes and in an instant, he had a face that looked like it had aged forty years. "Come to the car" were his only words.

Nathaniel led Karl into the drive way and he popped open the boot of his new car and nothing could prepare Karl for the sight he was about to see. There in the car boot was the fragile body of an obviously dead and mangled little girl. I dropped to my knees and as I looked up I saw Karl had done the same and as I covered my face with my hands and started to sob in the most gut wrenching uncontrollable sob that I had never even done while I was alive. I didn't even know ghosts could cry but in that one instant I felt the physical pain of my heart breaking for that child. Nathaniel was my own flesh and blood, but how could I comprehend and defend the actions of a man that had a dead child in his boot.

I had bought that car for him for doing well in school and university and it took every penny saved to get it. It was immaculate and clean and brand new when he drove it off the forecourt, and who would know that in its future its boot would have a beaten-up corpse of a child in it. There are no words for the devastation and the pain that I felt. The physical pain was gut wrenching, which was ironic for a woman with no physical body. If I could have died again I would have at that moment.

I decided to stand up and look closer at the little body in the car and I felt even more sick when I saw that it was the little mangled body of my new little companion, Katie Hoyland.

When Karl regained some sort of composure he grabbed Nathaniel by his shoulders and shook him. "What have you done" Karl said angrily. "Are you fucking drunk? Why were you driving? What have you done?"

Nathaniel was now sobbing and pacing round the room. "Honestly Karl" he said between gasps of sobs, "I was coming home down by the All Saints Social club and I swear to God she came out of nowhere"

"Why didn't you call an ambulance or anything, you absolute stupid boy" Karl replied, quite mild language for the situation in front of him I thought.

Nathaniel continued "I panicked and didn't know what to do. I don't want the police catching me drunk". By God was this my child! Nathaniel saw no problem in making it all about him apparently, typical child me, me, me. He really raised his voice to a shout and got right in Karl's face who was still sitting on the floor "I CAN'T HAVE THIS ON MY RECORD" and more quietly he whispered like a lost child "I had to bring her in case they found my car paint on her"

I stood there and watched in complete disbelief at what I was hearing. My child was a monster.

With a quick pulling together of senses, Nathaniel grabbed the top of the boot and slammed it closed. He then went to Karl to try and drag him up from the floor. "What shall I do? KARL WHAT SHALL I DO", Nathaniel was shouting.

Karl reluctantly got to his feet and immediately responded, "You, get you and that car to a police station

NOW!! You take your car and I will follow in mine because no doubt they are going to want your car". Nathaniel started crying and was pleading with Karl "I can't Karl, I can't, Mum will kill me, I am one year from graduating, and I can't do this"

Karl found his strength and grabbed Nathaniel by his neck in a choke hold. "You will go to a police station and take responsibility for your actions". And he threw Nathaniel in the car "NOW DRIVE". I think this is the one time Nathaniel has ever been scared of Karl as he started his engine, slammed his door and waited for Karl to get his keys to go.

I sat in Karl's car with him as we followed Nathaniel to the Copy Lane Police Station. Karl was livid but his anger was interrupted when his phone started ringing, it flashed up "Izzy Mob". He answered the phone to a very distressed alive version me who had a flat tyre on the way home from a gig and wanted to see if he could come and help me. After a quick exchange he took the address of where alive me was and put the phone down.

Outside the police station they both pulled up and got out of their cars. I passed through the car door to see Karl and Nathaniel stood by the boot of Nathaniel's car.

"Your mother needs my help. but I am telling you now, get into that police station and do the right thing"

Karl got in his car and drove off and I was left stood there looking at my confused son. However, no sooner had I closed my eyes to blink, I was whisked right back into the attic.

If Nathaniel had actually gone into the police station, why didn't he go to prison? There was no court cases that I knew of at the time and why was there still missing posters of Katie. From the information I remembered from Katie was that she said there were lots of missing posters after she went missing. Could Katie be wrong? She was wrong about her family moving away, could she be wrong about this.

I really didn't know how to process this information.

My son had killed a child. My baby had killed a baby.

Chapter 10 - Back to the Church

Back in the attic, I was in a rage. I didn't care how tired I was or the risk of being caught by the living, I wanted to get back to the church and let Tilly know my findings. I was crying and upset, angry, a whole load of emotions I had not even began to process yet. As I walked through the house the pictures moved like a strong wind passed them and I stormed out of the open front door with such a force that it closed behind me. Hope who'd ever had left it open had a spare key, however at this point, I really wasn't bothered about that.

I don't know how I got to the church so fast, however I got back to the church to find that Katie had been enjoying all the hijinks the church offered. She was going into vestibules and confession boxes listening to people's darkest confessions, which could have been anything from "wanting extra chocolate from the chocolate cupboard, to full on extra marital affairs. She was testing out her own spirit skills, as she dubbed them, seeing if she could press the keys on the massive church organ to make a noise. By the time I had arrived back, she had gone to sit outside to watch the world pass by.

When I eventually found Tilly, it was in a fit of tears that I unloaded all that I had found out to her. Needless to say, she was shocked and every now and then she would interrupt with a memory recall moment, she would pipe up with "come to think of it, I remember that missing girl" or "come to think of it, etc." After explaining everything, she was curious about what I had found out about Karl. "So did you find out how he died then?" In my haste I had forgotten that finding that out, was my main intention of the mission, however finding out my son had committed a death by drink driving had completely thrown me. With a great disappointment in my heart, I now knew that my son was a complete no mark of a human, but I wanted to and needed to know, if Karl had anything to do with it.

After a long discussion, and with the presence of Katie in our minds, Tilly and I decided that Katie should know about her family being alive, but not outright tell her how she died but give her an idea so as to not shock her. It was only then I would get back to trying to find my Karl and try clean up this whole mess.

Katie came running in, and it was quite possibly the most excited I had ever seen her. This girl really has missed having company in her long time in the spiritual world on her own. While looking at her face I was starting to wonder if she had lived in my attic for all this time for a reason, or whether she was actually a vengeful spirit looking for Nathaniel. Maybe I'm just thinking too much into it, and she really did just happen to come across my attic and liked living there. I was too cynical when I was alive to believe in coincidences, and even dead I am just as cynical. I saw her beautiful little face and yet the image from Nathaniel's car boot kept flashing back, her eyes open and blood in her hair.

In order to have this tentative conversation, we decided to start by sitting Katie down. This was completely new ground for me, the art of subtly, I was never that subtle in life and the same in death. I had raised Bella, I spoke to her, okay mostly like a mini adult, I could do this, I had to do this. Tilly and I sat down and I explained how I had visited her old address that I had found by remembering from her mirror vision. But I couldn't hold in my excitement and I just blurted out "I saw your Mum" I said. Katie on the other hand, didn't seem too enthusiastic, she glanced at me, and rolled her eyes. "Cool" was her rather subdued reply. Tilly and I looked at each other with a puzzled look on our faces, wondering why she seemed completely unimpressed with this information.

She gave a mini huff and said, "I am sorry, I kind of thought they were still there, I just made up the story cos I didn't want to see my Mum getting proper old". She went on to say" I stopped visiting a couple of years ago when my Mum got rid of my stuff and accepted I was dead, but I don't think I could have coped if she died, which is mad because I would see her again". We let her rabbit on for a couple more minutes about how she was awful sorry about lying and about how her older sister was doing her head in. Katie wasn't impressed with her older sister when she declared "She'd get more done if she wasn't too busy making her charity money about publicity for herself".

Me and Tilly sat there trying to listen and make sense of her rambling but it had occurred to me that my bubble had been burst about being the returning hero. It occurred to me that she had already told one little fib, what else had she not fully disclosed, I asked her out of curiosity "Katie, are you sure you don't know how you died?" She looked me right in the eye and said "I swear down, I don't know, but an old lady I used to sit with before she went up there told me that you never know how you die if its traumatic, it's mad that I even knew I was dead". This sparked my curiosity even more so I asked her to tell me more about the *" knowing you are dead"* thing.

She went on "well you see there's loads of lost souls just wandering round, sometimes you see them, sometimes you don't, and you just have to properly look. Well anyway, these people have usually died proper traumatic, like murdered or something like reeeaaalllly violent". This was interesting, it explained how she never remembered her death, but it never explained how she knew she was dead.

"Well I have been dead ages and I had a really good person looking after me. She said she was my Mum's Nanna and told me I had '*passed* away', said it proper nice like. It took me ages to believe her to be honest. She was really nice and taught me a lot of my tricks I know today. She said she had already been to the other place and came back to look after me". I was surprised at the length of the conversation we were having; she only usually spoke in small rushed sentences. Katie continued "The day my Mum said she knew I was dead, then my Nanna went back to her other place".

I had heard references to this Other Place but never really understood it, so I asked Katie what it was and that appeared to be one question too much for Katie as she ran back off citing that she had things to do, people to see.

Oh to be young free and dead.

I wasn't going to ruin her freedom by telling her how she died. Young Katie had died a death that would traumatise anyone. As resilient as she was turning out to be, I decided that this would be too much. This was my son who did this to this girl and now it was my unfinished business, not hers.

It had all made me think that maybe all the things that Katie was saying was the reason I hadn't found my Karl. What if she knew how he had died? Was it traumatic or was he actually dead at all? Was he one of the lost souls lost somewhere waiting for a guide to show him the way? There was only one way to find out but today was not that day. I needed to organise my thoughts and rest. I would have to try to banish the image of the young body mangled in my son's car. Even though I will hold that guilt every time I see that ghost child's face, that for her sake, I will try push it to the back of my mind, I would attempt to enjoy the sunshine with Tilly and a very happy Katie, to try and enjoy my after-life.

Chapter 11 - Organised thoughts and answers to new questions.

After a night of rest, I woke up and I wanted to know more. I needed to know what my son was thinking when he decided to drive drunk and put a dead child in his car boot, instead of ring the police to the scene. I wanted to know why there was no court case that I knew about, or if it was the case that Nathaniel did in fact go to the police station. I had to look back to my memories.

Without using a mirror as a memory aid, I remembered that at the time there were more newspapers than usual in the house. Since about 2010, Karl never really used physical newspapers, and mainly got his news from various social media sites and online, so to see these papers was slightly unusual, but not 'alarm bell' unusual. I also remembered that Nathaniel had gone back to University early without telling me face to face. It wasn't unusual for him to text me and his text in this instance simply said "gone back to campus, going to Ibiza with lads before term starts". I was busy looking after my Bella and trying to forge a cabaret career to think that this was out of character.

I felt a ghostly tear down my face. It was because of my own self-involvement that led to the fact that I didn't know that my son had killed another human being, and my heart was broken. I was trying to think rational in order to try and get to the bottom of this, however every now and then I felt a prang of pain to my heart and it reminded me that I could have done something if I was only paying attention.

This was all I couldn't remember, I needed Karl's mirror to unpick this whole series of events, I needed to see what he was doing. It was a shame you couldn't see memories of the living in one of their mirrors as Nathaniel's brain needed picking and the secrets he had hidden away needing exposing.

I was about to go back to the house, but on leaving the church I bumped into Tilly. "You are looking tired there Izzy, Should you be putting this much effort into this?" She had a point, people were alive and able to try and put pieces together. However, this was an injustice that appeared to slip under the livings radar. I didn't set out trying to find out what my son did, I just wanted to find my Karl and if it means following this path then so be it. Tilly seemed satisfied with my response but warned "be careful, as you age here your soul rots, you don't want to be walking round like a zombie with no brains in the spirit world, like *that one* there"

That one? "What are you talking about" I asked as I looked where she pointed into an empty space in the corner by the pew. "Look closer" she said, and then I saw her. A really see through woman sitting on the step. Her face was stuck like that abstract Robert Munsch's *Scream* painting. The space where her eyes should have been were white. She wasn't doing much, just sitting there lost, her hair waiving round like she was trapped under water. It was quite haunting and a little bit scary, even to an adult. It was a little intriguing however there was something really sad about her.

I had decided to ignore the advice of Tilly, so I convinced both of them to come to my old house to see the pandemonium of Joe and the baby preparation. Tilly wasn't up for seeing that mayhem, but she did say she would take Katie back to her old house, if Katie wanted to.

I wanted to go back to see Karl's mirror but didn't want Tilly to know that's what I was intending on doing. Even though the image of the lost ghost in the church still stuck in my head, I didn't feel that I was at that scary lady's point yet! It was a lovely day as I strolled towards the house. Katie and Tilly had decided to keep me company until we got to the crossroads by where Katie had lived. I told Tilly I just wanted to go see my family and although she rolled her eyes and knew what I was really up to, she seemed to let it go, with a parting words of "be careful".

Katie, sensing the slight tension between myself and Tilly, suddenly blurted out "I think I want to go see my Mum now". Tilly turned and faced her and said "Are you sure you are ready?" said Tilly cautiously but kind as usual. Katie reminded Tilly "I have been a ghost a lot longer than you, if you think I can't handle it then maybe you should come with me". We looked at each other a little taken back, and Tilly nodded as if to say "I've got this".

I split off from Tilly and Katie, and watched them nattering as they travelled down the road towards Katie's previous home. As I turned to face the other way, there was a red sports car which was coming down the road at great speed, which for a suburban area, the speed should have been less than twenty miles per hour, but this car was definitely doing at least forty. It slowed down slightly at the cross roads and I could see that it was Kate, Katie's niece and namesake. It got me thinking, if Kate knew how her aunt died, would she be driving so fast. As I was stood in the middle of the road, the car passed right through me and felt rather unusual to say the least. You know the feeling like you have been winded and the breath taken out of you, well that's sort of what it felt like. In the past when I have passed through objects or they have passed through me, it has never felt like this. It started me thinking that maybe Tilly was right, my spirit wasn't coping well with all this activity.

I got to the old house and I went straight back to the attic to look in Karl's mirror. I was adamant that I needed to find answers and what more my Karl knew about my son and his crime. What I really wanted to know was why he didn't follow up the lack of apparent trial. I looked into his mirror.

Through the mirror, I was transported to my living room. I could hear an alive and happier version of me hollering upstairs, singing my songs and pottering round cleaning and organising. Downstairs I could see Karl with his pile of newspapers, pens and post it notes. There were also a few missing posters of young girls on the pile of papers, one for Katie, which had a few sheets of blank music staves just enough to cover it. He had a hard backed note book next to him where he was making notes. I decided to have a sneak over his shoulder and have a look at his notes that he was frantically scribbling. Inside the book he had stuck the various missing posters with different missing children, noting their age and location. On the front page he had a map with dots and circles, which from the looks of it, Karl was looking at these missing children in the radius of our home. I could have sworn blind that Karl was playing investigator. As the alive version of me came down the stairs he quickly slammed his book shut and covered the papers with his various blank music staves, alien books and paraphernalia.

Alive Isabelle was on her way out, as she was frantically looking for keys, purse, glasses and her handbag. Karl exchanged a few pleasantries with alive me as he always did, usually along the lines of what my errands for the day were. Just like clockwork, as always, he kissed me on my forehead as me and Bella toddled out the door. Just before the live me closed the door, he said "have you heard how Nathaniel is doing?", The alive version of me, obviously flustered with trying to leave the house with a child and bags under my arms said "not since his text telling me he's gone back to Uni, you know him, he's a pain in the arse when it comes to keeping in touch, I just leave him to it." Alive me slammed the door as she bid her farewell and Karl got back to his scribblings. It was obvious to see from his scrawling's that he had discovered the missing girl Katie Hoyland, matched the location and age and time of disappearance, of the one in Nathaniel's boot. I saw him pick up his mobile and try and call Nathaniel. I could see from his phone he had tried to call him fifty-six times over god knows how many days. Nathaniel's phone went straight to voicemail and I think just like spirit me, Karl had realised that when he left Nathaniel at the police station, he didn't hand himself in.

I could see it in his eyes, I had seen this face many a time with Karl. He had decided enough was enough. He grabbed his book and started a fresh page. He began to write his findings, his version of events with the sentence starter, "To Merseyside Police". I could only assume that he was going to gather this "evidence" to go and report it to the police as an anonymous tip off. I could see his reasoning, feel what he was thinking, so late on after the event, he thought it had been too long for him to go and confess to knowing, without getting accused of aiding and abetting a criminal. He had the added complication that it was my son; he was hiding the heartache from me. He wrote the letter but when it came to the part where he wrote about seeing the body, he realised without a body he couldn't give anyone closure and police would probably treat the letter as not serious. I was frustrated with him, oh why wouldn't he just let the police do their job and stop assuming? He used to tell me off for assuming all the time!

He scribbled a sort of *confession by proxy* for Nathaniel but he needed to find the little girl's body. He sealed the letter in an envelope and kept it in his scrap book. He walked into the kitchen and started to make himself a cup of tea and out the corner of his eye, he saw a sat nav sitting in the see-through plastic draws looking at him. I could see his thought process, had Nathaniel used it that night? And if so is there a "last places visited" option.

Karl grabbed the sat nav and his bag with his notes in and ran to his car, I know that he would take the letter direct to the police station if he was to find a body. The sat nav was that old it would only hold a charge in the car cigarette lighter socket. He plugged it in and turned it on. He was panicking, why it would be in the kitchen and not in the car Nathaniel was driving that night. It was common knowledge that Nathaniel wasn't good at giving borrowed items back.

But then I remembered that the previous summer, I had to get a train to some festival that Nathaniel had driven to, but he had to abandon the car, as he was off his face on whatever drugs were available. I had to drive using the sat nav to get home, and popped it back into the kitchen storage draws.

Karl never knew about any of Nathaniel's failings from that summer, as it was clear they were not getting along. Karl had a mission and he had to try to forget his own cynicism and just hope that the sat nav had his answers. When in the car, he switched the sat nav on, however it wasn't switching on fast enough for my impatient husband. "Come on, come on" he whispered to himself. As it switched on, he quickly got to the "places navigated to" page. On the list, about nine places down, was one that was a little out of place between the places in distant counties, this one was more local; it was directions to Delemere forest. Karl knew it wasn't him who had searched for this destination, as he travelled up there so often that he didn't need a sat nav. Secondly, the place that Karl had seen on the sat nav was nowhere near where he would usually go. With this new information, Karl planned a trip up to Delemere in the next holiday.

I came out of Karl's mirror memory for a second. I remembered the time after this and the holiday he went on, I remembered it well as this was his last trip I ever saw him. At the time he insisted that Bella and I stay at home as she wasn't very well. I can't believe I was so caught up with trying to keep the family afloat and organised that I didn't notice any of this, any of his research and investigations. I have never considered myself to be a naïve person but by the way this whole diabolical was unfolding I was questioning my sanity on how I had managed to miss such a massive event. I started to cry again, not cry, sob. In my head I kept saying to myself "snap out of it, you're dead you can't be sad in your afterlife!" but then it all came flooding back to a realisation that my child had killed someone else's child and I couldn't *rest in peace* as they say, until I had solved this.

Over the years, Karl had visited Delemere many times as despite his "rock and roll persona, he had an avid interest in all things *Extra Terrestrial,* and Delemere was, in his words, a hot spot for interplanetary 'shenanigans'. It was the one thing that we completely disagreed on. Whenever I criticised the idea of aliens, his standard response was, "pft, it's arrogant to think we are the only intelligent life in the vast universe". So, to him, Delemere, in his opinion, was a buzzing hive of UFO activity. Any opportunity he got to go up there he went up. At first, I had always assumed that there was another woman, always convinced he had traded me in for a younger model. His obsession with going to that woodland caused many an argument. However, I don't know now what was worse at this present moment, the thought of my husband running off with another woman or my child being a killer.

I decided to have a sleep before I looked in the mirror again, but while I slept my memories manifested in my dreams. I saw Nathaniel come home from University and graduate. I also saw the constant arguments he and Karl had, as they did not get along. It got so bad that at one point, they weren't allowed near each other at family events. Even at baby Lucy's christening, Karl and I left shortly after Nathaniel and his brash mouthy wife began making sly jibes at Karl's music career and his obsession with UFO's. I will always remember the comment Karl made to Nathaniel whereby he reminded Nathaniel that having a baby will only keep him out of prison so long. I had always thought he was referring to his fraud case, never would I have thought it would involve this little girl's death.

I had finally accepted that I had raised a monster.

Chapter 12 - The Journey Ahead

Feeling fresher after my sleep, I stepped back into Karl's mirror and I was transported to many years later. I saw the alive me waving off Karl as he went *"asteroid and alien light spotting"* in Delemere forest. I decided that I should jump in the car with Karl and see where his investigation was going.

In the car, I was sat next to my beautiful husband watching the world go by as we drove, from my memory banks I recalled the events that I knew that happened at the time. I remember that not more than half an hour after Karl had gone, Nathaniel had turned up at mine, just for a cuppa tea. I was expecting him, as the twenty minutes before he had done his usual phone call to check if Karl was there first so he could sit with me and gossip about any new family news.

Nathaniel told me he was going on a road trip with Lucy and was wondering if he could borrow the family sat nav. I had told him that Karl had just literally taken it with him up to Delemere. I had wondered why he didn't just use his smart phone GPS, but Nathaniel had just said "err good idea, thanks Mum, see you soon". He took Lucy by the hand and out of the house back to the car. I could have shaken myself, what an oblivious stupid naïve Mum.

If I knew then that this would be the last time that I saw my husband, 'alive me' would have jumped in the car with him. The benefit of hindsight would be a great thing

He had the sat nav attached to his screen and I saw him pick the Delemere forest destination and make a bit of a risky U-turn to follow it. During the long journey I was sure he could sense my presence, or maybe I just wanted him to sense it. This was because sometimes I swear he was looking right at me in the seat next to him. I wish I could touch him. He had done this journey a million times, but I could see from the destination screen that it was taking him to a particular spot at the other side of the forest. In the back seat were his note books with maps and the letter he wrote that was now crumpled. There were small tears in the papers and the brown staining from excessive handling of the documents with his hands, it looks like he had been working on this for years.

It wasn't the busiest road that he was on, but as I glanced back, I saw that there seemed to be the same car behind him a couple of times and Karl had never noticed. Was it the same car or was it me being paranoid? Silver was probably the most common colour for cars nowadays. I think his need to investigate has turned me paranoid.

Once you get past the industrial scenes of Runcorn, the drive thereafter is actually quite picturesque. I have this theory that in life you are either a seaside person or a woodland person. In that you either enjoy the tranquillity of the coast and the water, or that you were more of an earthy nature person. In Karl's' younger years, he made us live by the coast most of our lives, he was definitely a seaside person. It was the lure of his "Ufology" and the search for intelligent life" that drove Karl to the woodland and more inland areas. He truly believed that "according to research", most alien sightings were in forests and woodland. He used to take us camping with him, until I got fed up of being second best to the lights in the sky. I quite enjoyed my home comforts, a non-lumpy bed, a shower and the ability to sit on a toilet rather than have wet legs behind a shrub. He had always promised us a camper home whenever we got a bit of money, so that we could enjoy the home comforts while being able to follow the lights. We just never got round to it and always had better things to spend money on.

Suddenly, "In three hundred yards, you have reached your destination" the sat nav rang out. This confused Karl as it wasn't a car park or any of the more known about entrances to the park. It was quite an isolated place. He parked in a nook on the side of the road, and brought his books and a metal detector kit he had stashed in the boot. He saw a recently trodden path that wasn't a proper path and he decided to follow it. I was behind him looking at the trees and the foliage. As I walked, I could hear the leaves and twigs made a noise underfoot. I didn't know why and it was freaking me out, I shouldn't be able to make noise in memories, my tiredness and transitioning to a solid form shouldn't happen in these memories. Luckily Karl didn't notice it, he looked back occasionally but was looking right through me. It got me thinking though, were those breaking twig noises my footsteps, they couldn't be Karl's as he was about forty feet ahead of me. They must have been mine, unless there was someone following us. My mind flashed back to that silver car.

I ran to catch up with him as he marched on. As he approached a clearing there was nothing remarkable about it. It was probably one of the only places he hadn't looked at in the past twenty-five years since the young girl, Katie had gone missing; no not missing, murdered. He looked around, he knew what he was looking for, uneven ground, rocks that didn't looked out of place, anything. He got his metal detector out of its bag and put his bulky over ear headphones on. That's when I saw Nathaniel. Karl was so intently listening and looking at the ground searching that he didn't notice Nathaniel was coming through the thick of the forest. I ran up to Nathaniel in an attempt to stop him approaching, then ran up to Karl to try and attempt in vain to warn him. Nathaniel wasn't dressed appropriately for a walk in the forest and if I remember rightly five-year-old Lucy was in the car with him when he came to mine that day. Was he with her now? Had he left her in the car?

Then I saw it in his hand, it was a crowbar and he was walking right behind an unsuspecting man that was my husband. He didn't stand a chance. Every swipe I took as he raise the crow bar over an unsuspecting Karl, went right through it. I saw him crack Karl on the head with the sharp end of the crowbar. It got stuck and buried into his head, I was screaming "stop". Karl fell forward then turned around. He looked Karl in the eye and simply said "you got too close old man".

With those parting words, Nathaniel had released the crowbar from his skull and continued to beat Karl round the face and round the head with this metal iron. Until all was left was a twitching body of my husband I couldn't help but scream. I was inconsolable I dropped to the ground and suddenly was taken out of the forest back into the attic.

In front of me stood a shocked Tilly and Katie who had returned from Katie's Mum's house. I cried and sobbed and fell to the floor. I couldn't believe it, accidently killing a child in the car was bad enough, but Nathaniel could have done the right thing, but he didn't, it would appear he's buried her in the woods and Karl was just about to find her. But now a brutal violent murder of my soul mate, my one true love. The fruit of my womb was a monster and my husband was now presumably a lost soul trying to do the right thing. I would rather he was having an affair!!!!

After a massive group hug from my companions I told them what I had learned right from the beginning. It was a spur of the moment decision to tell Katie how she had died, and I wish I had found the strength to be that bit more delicate when broaching the subject, but I was absolutely traumatised. I wish I could drink right now. Katie had a better suggestion in order to alleviate some of this rage I was feeling. Joe the Oaf was in on his own in the kitchen experimenting with baking "skins onto his model figurines". In a blink of an eye we were all downstairs, and in my extremely tired state, I started picking up the dishes in the rack. It didn't take a lot of concentration because of how intense my last mirror journey was, so I simply picked it up and dropped it on the floor. Joe jumped a mile out of his skin knocking his models to the floor. I then started throwing dishes indiscriminately against the wall.

Katie then joined in. However my sense of shame took over, I wasn't having this. I had just seen my husband murdered and my only way to relieve the stress was pranking a dope of a man? No! I need to get revenge, I needed my son to know he wasn't getting away with this despite the fact he had evaded the authorities for so long. My thoughts were stopped by Katie screaming while looking at me. Tilly shouted "oh my god what's happening to you". I looked into the microwave reflective surface. My eyeballs had gone black, like the soulless zombies. Ahhh shit. "This has to stop" Tilly said, look at you, you are losing your light, you look haggard and just look at your eyes. Stop while your senses are about you, you need sleep so let me and Katie find somewhere to rest.

We hadn't the energy to get back to the church so the attic in my near visible state, it was. I climbed in the corner and slept like a log. Katie was whispering lullabies which turned into some sort of foreign language in my ear as I was drifting off. It was familiar but comforting. I am sure I have drifted off to the same whispers after my Karl went missing. It was comforting to know my little companion was probably with me in life, and probably knew more about me that I knew about myself.

Chapter 12 ½ - Reawakening

I woke with a start and also alone, as Tilly and Katie appeared to have deserted me. I have never slept so soundly even in life. Katie's words and whispers must have been like tramadol for the dead. Katie and Tilly appeared from the same corner the mirror was in. Katie's voice chirped up, "Look Tilly she's awake". Tilly came over and hugged me "we thought you would never wake up! You have been asleep for three whole weeks, you look so much better". Oh my, the investigations and the trauma of my last mirror visit had obviously taken a toll on my soul. I looked into Karl's mirror and this time instead of the swirls, it showed my reflection. I looked thirty-eight again.

Tilly and Katie had so much to share with me. She had been to her Mums but hadn't learned anything there however, she enjoyed seeing her sisters as old women and was happy she had nieces who were named after her and so pretty. They had spent some time observing her niece Kate sitting and following her round. She was a popular young lady, drove a lovely car and had a lovely boyfriend. Unfortunately as with most young people around her age, she also had taste for alcohol and some of the old 'Columbian marching powder' – cocaine. She was studying sociology in university, and hadn't planned any sort of career past that. She adored her Grandma, but also adored sneaking the odd tenner out of her Grandmother's purse when she wasn't looking.

Katie's Mum pretended she never noticed the money going missing, and this upset Katie as this was when she saw her mum as a broken woman, she had lost her fight when her daughter died and just kind of let injustices roll over her head.

With Karl's saga, Tilly and Katie had took up in Karl's mirror where I had left off. Tilly told me that they had watched Nathaniel dig a hole with the spade that Karl had bought, once the whole was big enough he put Karl in it, went back to his car and put all the maps and things in the hole with him. They had checked the car that Nathaniel had come in and there was a child in the car asleep. I concluded that this must have been Lucy. Nathaniel drove Karl's car further into the woodland in the hope that no one would ever find it. He then drove home in his own car and he dumped the crowbar in the pond in his back garden and finally got a shower using bleach as shower gel. He explained his red raw skin to his wife as an allergy to the new fabric softener the laundrette had been using. I didn't understand how they could see Nathaniel's memories as he was alive and Karl was dead so they certainly wasn't Karl's memories. Maybe they are the memories of Karl's ghost. We were entering paradoxes now that I couldn't get my head round.

Even after having had a long sleep and time to calm down, I couldn't help it that I was still angry, upset and tearful, but I could think rationally now. I didn't know how I was going to direct anyone to there but I remembered that Lucy wanted to visit Delemere forest. I was wondering if there was a way I could direct her there, to that particular spot. Tilly could see my brain ticking over, and with a sudden start she shouted " NOW STOP, you have your answers, we can go to Delemere to try find Karl but it's not your job to do the rest." She was really angry now and I had never seen her like this ever, alive or dead. She continued "look at how you went, we nearly lost you". She really did have a point. We needed to watch the world go by for a bit. I knew my Karl was dead, so he's either gone to his "Other Place" or he wondering around lost for the past fifteen years, or doing what I was doing in trying to get revenge. Yes I had answers but not enough. I think from now on my investigations wouldn't be shared with Tilly or Katie and I would get this done on my own.

After years of watching ghost hunting program and the various theories that exist about parapsychology, I used to laugh and pooh pooh the existence of ghosts and vengeful spirits. I could see in my short time in the afterlife that I had been all of the terrible cliché's that the wacky ghost expert presenters had talked about.

Chapter 14 -Mulling over

Having those visible results of how tired I had become, it had been decided to settle and rest for a whole week back in the church, wasn't that much to note about this week, we spoke, we rested, we cried and we laughed. Katie appeared completely unfazed by the fact I had told her how she died, either she really wasn't bothered or she had a really good poker face. There's not a lot to do when you are dead, and especially when your minder has forced you to not do anything. I was patient for a while but I can't just sit here, as I've never been one to sit on my thumbs. What's more frustrating is that there's not even anything to do, such as reading books, for the simple fact they are physical and you can't turn the pages without using excessive amounts of concentration. For need of a better word, the afterlife is shit and I am totally convinced that there has to be more to it than this. I have been the cinema and watched some of the new films that are out and am getting annoyed that everything is sequels, prequels and comic book remakes. I got so fed up and bored that I decided to ignore Tilly's advice and have a visit to the old house. I knew Lucy was going to Delemere soon so I may as well go with her even if it's just to kill some time.

I assured Tilly that I wasn't going to investigate anymore, and that I just wanted to see the place and if he happened to be there then so be it. She knew I was lying but reluctantly agreed to let me go on my own, but only because she realised that there was no convincing me that this was anyone's responsibility but mine to deal with. I went to the old house hoping she was going the same day but when I got there, I saw that there was some packing done but not enough justify them going yet. I was as impatient in death as I was in life. I wish I could rush them along and get through to the two of them, my burning sense of urgency. I had seen my Karl die and knew how it finished for him. I just wanted him back in my arms. At least he was on my spirit plane of existence and not living in a nursing home with a memory loss ailment such as dementia, in a body that no longer works.

While I was waiting, I just kind of skulked round the house watching people come and go. Joe the Oaf was still entertaining me with his sheer idiotic behaviour, but for some reason I was feeling less resentment towards him and was actually warming to him. I felt that if I was with them as a live person, I would be laughing with him instead of at him. But the more I watched, the more his childish behaviour came out, and I still felt that he was clearly not ready to be a father. I have been proven wrong before, and I hope he can prove me wrong once these babies are born. Lucy's bump was really starting to show now, so I was wondering whether she should be going camping, or was it my hatred of camping that was making me feel this way.

Since the last time I had been to the old house, she had two scan pictures on the mantelpiece, one in a blue frame and one in a pink frame. Not being daft and not one to point out the obvious, I had assumed this meant her babies were one girl and one boy. On the wall there was a chalk board with two columns. The first one label "boy" and second one labelled "girl". Underneath were chalk writing scrawls for different ideas for names. Joe's guesses were obvious... Link and Sonic for boys and Zelda or Lara for a girl, he did love his retro game names. It was lovely and refreshing to see the pair of them in their natural environment, not knowing they were being watched. Joe in all of his stupidity, he really did love my granddaughter. There was no job to big or small that he wouldn't do. Most importantly he made sure she was fed and had her feet up all the time. Seeing their little idiosyncrasies on how they interacted made me smile. Like how Joe uses the corner of a wardrobe to scratch the top of his back and Lucy would always say "just like Baloo", making a reference to a really old cartoon called *The Jungle Book*. It was sweet and caring, and reminded me of the private times between me and Karl when we were younger.

During the days I watched them talk and rest, of a night I would sleep on the old sofa in the front room. It was a nice feeling being around them, but on the other hand it was so utterly sad at the same time. I so wanted to be alive and be a part of this baby excitement. Then the day came, a day I was dreading, the day that I would see Nathaniel's face knowing what he had done.

 Nathaniel had come to visit one day with Lucy's mother, and I can honestly say I have never felt so much hatred in my life (death?). I took a deep breath, as I promised Tilly I wouldn't get wound up, because there was nothing I could do about it now. I watched how he made sly digs and jibes at Joe, and also less harsh, but still equally hurtful comments to Lucy. I also noticed how Lucy's mother was barely recognisable with the amount of plastic surgery she had. I don't think there was any more saggy skin left to staple back into her head. She looked positively terrifying.

Obviously my inheritance was being spent on Rodney Street in Liverpool, Plastic Alley. Listening into the conversation I could hear him again saying, "why are you going to Delemere when you are so close to giving birth. You could go at any time". I knew now why he was so reluctant to let her go and I was spitting feathers. I got less than a centimetre from his face and said "you horrible little bastard, I know why you don't want her to go". Okay, he couldn't hear me but I felt better saying it. I was quite relieved to hear Lucy reply that she was going tomorrow and that when she gets back its pure relaxation until the babies were born.

I was absolutely seething so I went to a spare room and found a bed to lie on until tomorrow. I can't risk anyone seeing me tomorrow because it's going to be a long day.

****

The next day, the whole house was awake early, I could hear Lucy scurrying round the kitchen so I went downstairs. She was busy pottering around and was putting together a cool box with food. Joe was in the garden collapsing the tent after he had attempted to put it up and put it down in the back garden. When they were ready to go Lucy sat in the car while Joe loaded up all the heavy things in the newly hired seven seater van. I noticed something odd sticking to the windscreen; it was the old family sat nav from all those years ago. Of course! When Tilly had finished seeing what the memory version of Nathaniel was up to, she wouldn't have noticed that Nathaniel had took the Sat Nav back out of Karl's car. She wouldn't have realised how important it was to the murder.

Joe's inability to drive and lack of driving licence meant the weight of driving a heavily laden car, went to my equally heavy-laden granddaughter. The first thing she did was open the sat nav and use the previous history to go to a similar destination I had seen not so long ago in Karl's mirror.

On the drive there Joe asked her "why do you want to come here?" Lucy replied, "Me and my Dad used to come here quite a lot, sometimes just to sit, sometimes just to walk, but it helped me get over Grandad Karl going missing". I scowled, my son the cheeky, sneaky and sick little shit. He took his daughter to the scene of the crime where he bludgeoned her grandfather to death and buried him. Was he taking the piss?

Deep   breaths   Isabelle.……...one……. two…….
three……. I won't get wound up

I listened to them jabber and chatter for the whole journey to Delemere. They laughed, they got angry when Lucy cut up someone in the middle lane of the motorway, then two seconds later they were friends again. My first opinion of Joe was changing. These two were made for each other and there wasn't much that could separate them. These babies will either make them or break them and now I am hoping that they make them. They haven't had an easy time at all despite being able to live in my old house rent free. At least the money wasn't being spent by Nathaniel, well until he found an excuse to kick them out to sell the house. The way his wife is nip tucking her face, she may need the money to start replacing other parts of herself.

The sat nav gave off its now hauntingly familiar voice. "In three hundred yards you have reached your destination" as they pulled up to the point on the map. It was a destination I recognised from the mirror and I felt the anger was brewing but this time it was tainted with an utter sadness. They stopped, pulled over and identified their camping spot and I watched as Lucy and Joe get to work on unloading her car. Joe set about setting up the tent. I reckon that they needed at least an eight-man tent, due to the amount of stuff they had. They had a double off-the-ground camp bed, cooking stoves, generator and a mini fridge. All the comforts of home but in a tent. Camping had evolved since I last went into the great outdoors, as "Glamping" had just started to take off. I had decided that even with the home comforts I was too old to keep sleeping outdoors so I decided to stop.

The only thing I missed about giving up camping was the outdoor cooking. I loved making soups and fry ups, the BBQ's and salads. Although the food was my favourite part, I also liked sunbathing, the burning camp fire and even loved the fishing. I especially loved the peace and quiet. However when it came to sleeping in the outdoors and having no clean bathroom facilities, sleeping outdoors when I had cosy central heating at home just seemed like utter insanity. The thought of creepy spiders crawling into my mouth knocked me sick. One time we went with just our dog at the time, Alfie. The dog, also being used to sleeping indoors in a cosy house, got all freaked out when it started to rain, so me and the dog ended up sleeping in the car. I swear I've had a twinge in my back ever since.

Lucy was being waited on hand and foot after Joe had put up the tent. Lucy had the mini barbeque on with some sausages and burgers. The little table she was using next to her was being used to chop up a salad. Bless her, she wasn't a natural cook, but the barbeque suited her natural "burn everything" style of cooking. They were having fun talking and laughing, holding conversations instead of being tied to electronic devices and screens. All phones were in the car, they didn't want the electronic distraction, but recognising Lucy's risky pregnancy and being far from home, he kept it in the car and accessible. This was bliss for these two, to the point that I had started to feel like a third wheel, so decided to have a wander into the forest.

I knew they were camping not far from the spot that Tilly had seen Nathaniel bury my husband, so I went to go and see what was there now.

With a strange feeling of Déjà vu, the feelings were similar to the ones I was feeling when in Karl's mirror. Again, I didn't know why but I could feel the twigs crunching underneath my feet when I was meant to be weightless and flowing. I know I wasn't as tired this time, or maybe I was and feel it. As I wandered through the trees and I saw it, the sunken ground where they were under. It was obvious that someone had been here recently topping the sunken bit of land with topsoil and scattering leaves over it. This was because the newer soil was darker and more disturbed.

There was a sort of twisted irony of the site of Karl's final resting place. About seven months before he died, Karl had bought a double plot in a natural woodland burial ground, as he would have loved the idea of having his final resting place in a woodland. Perhaps though without the gruesome bludgeoned death that came with it.

It was for a little while that I was just sitting and just contemplating my afterlife that I saw something from the corner of my eye. I stood up and started to walk round the area to see if I could catch it. Then I saw it looking lifeless and zombie like stood by a tree and I couldn't believe my eyes, was it really? It couldn't be.

It was my Karl. I ran right up to him and shouted his name.

I say my Karl, however it wasn't my Karl, it was one of them lost soul ghosts I had seen at the church that time. My Karl had been transformed into one. I tried to say hello and, in my frustration, I found myself shouting "look at me, can you hear me". He was just not having it. He looked right through me and just wandered round the trees. I followed him for a bit and every now and then there were more of them just appearing, like they had been there all along, but only appeared when I was ready to see them.

The temperature had suddenly dropped and a thick mist had formed, there was a heavy depressed feeling about the area. The trees were suddenly closer to each other and floating past were random faces and lots of these strange ghosts. If I had flesh arms, am pretty sure the hairs on them would be stood up. I was scared. I couldn't believe that I had come so close to being one of these with my obsession with finding the truth.

Different spirits were just wandering round aimlessly, looking exactly as that strange woman in the church. Their eyes were all white and they were sort of gliding around slowly, in a way which made them look like they were floating. Very eerie, surreal and scary as I walked through the barrage of spirits. Is this where the ghosts come to die, even more so than they already were? I aimlessly followed Karl through the sea of floating ghosts until he started to wander back to where his burial spot was. He just sat down. That wasn't my husband, I didn't know what that was but I needed to find out so I could spend my eternity with him.

I sat there with him, just looking at his blank face for what seemed like a couple of hours. My peace was suddenly disturbed. I heard someone behind me say "are you not scared? As I turned around quickly, I saw my older self in ghost form stood there. You would think that I would be freaked out, looking at myself, but she wasn't me, she just looked like me. I don't even know how I knew that wasn't me, I just knew.

"This is where the ghosts come who have become exhausted" Old me said, answering the question I was about to ask. "Exhausted?" I asked. "Yes, exhausted, like tired". Older me rudely shot back. She rolled her eyes "see all the running round you have been doing, nearly getting caught in mirrors, trying to find *'your beloved husband';* she said with her nose turned up and in a sarcastic manner. "well" she continued "this is what happens, they either get stuck in a corner somewhere or they are that beyond tired they come to me to wonder round somewhere they are less likely to get caught by the living".

Okay so this made some sort of sense, but didn't make it any less eerie. I was looking at myself telling me that someone who looked like me was some sort of guardian for lost souls. It was a bit of a mind bend to say the least.

"Why do you look like me?" I asked a little hesitantly. Again older me rolled her eyes in a way that got me thinking, maybe now I know why people got a little intimidated when I got irate; *'if looks could kill'* and all that. "Do I look like you?, I am not you, I just have to try and adapt to a image you won't get scared of, and if I look like you, then clearly you were one of the only people you weren't scared off, bit narcissistic if you ask me though Sweetie." This was not a pleasant person, either that or she was someone who had a hard job to do and didn't have time to answer the same questions over again.

I got the feeling her patience was wearing thin, I thought I would only try to press her one more time, but before I could ask anything, she jumped in first "So are you wanting to know what's going on with this sorry sack sitting here?" she pointed at Karl. "Well that would be nice to know", I replied a little snippier. "This man here was a regular visitor here, don't ask me why, he'd go missing for days, weeks and years then come back again. Then one day he turned into one 'of them". As she said "of them" she tilted her head and eyes towards the other lost souls wondering around.

I glanced in the directions of the other souls and when I came back to her, she had gone. I wasn't completely satisfied with her response but what could I do? I sat next to my lost soul husband for a while to see if my presence would bring him round. After all, Tilly and Kate had fixed me when I nearly turned.

Eventually Karl stood up and turned towards the other souls and he entered the mist and disappeared. After my experience I decided it was probably best that I went back to the place where Lucy and Joe were camping. When I got there, they were already snuggled up in bed. I thought that I might as well try and re-live the Alfie camping experience, and try have a sleep in the car.

The next morning, I was grouchy, noting that this was exactly how I woke up the last time I slept in the car. I had nightmares about the faces in the forest. Lucy was up and about trying to find a nice tree to have a wee behind, all quite uncomfortable knowing her bump was getting bigger. They spent the morning pottering around and cleaning up the site and then themselves. After they had done their business she went wandering with Joe in the direction of the place that I knew as the burial spot. He had a wheelbarrow of what appeared to be instant light charcoal and peat, and Lucy carried a massive hunk of meat in a plastic bag. I heard them talking:-

"Listen Babe" Joe said, "I totally saw it on this cooking program where some fella from a posh estate basically digs a hole in the ground, starts the peat bonfire, then puts a bit of soil on it then lashes the meat in the hole, wrapped in tinfoil and a burlap sack" he was salivating with excitement. Lucy, like myself looked confused and said, "yeah but doesn't soil put fire out? I'm sure it needs oxygen to burn and it isn't burning with soil on it". Science was always her strong point. "yeah but the beauty is that the peat is supposed to go on fire and keep the heat and you set another fire on top of it and that way it cooks the meat" Joe finished. Lucy looked completely unconvinced by this whole escapade but as usual was willing to let him try, after all, what's the worst that can happen?

Part of me started to get weirdly excited as I saw the shovel hit the ground exactly where the two bodies were buried. Part of me was wondering how Joe, the one I had utterly no faith in and watched him do the most idiotic things, was slowly becoming the hero of this whole piece. I was actively cheering him on "come on son DIIIIIIGGGGGGGG". He stopped and I was a little perplexed as to why "ahh girl, me backs gone you know, do you fancy grabbing that trowel and having a go" Joe moaned. First Lucy laughed and then she realised he was deadly serious. Good old Joe, totally gone from hero to zero, the work-shy weirdo.

Lucy reluctantly climbed down the hole with her little trowel, while Joe climbed out to go crack open a beer he had stashed in his wheelbarrow. I am sure I brought that girl up to have a little more backbone, that way she would be able to tell Joe to sling his hook, or maybe she inherited her father's jelly spine.

She sat there happily but uncomfortably, scrapping away the soil when she came across a plastic bag embedded in the soil. She turned to Joe, "Joe, what's this? Do you reckon someone has already had your idea about cooking meat underground already?" Joe went to the edge of the hole and started to help Lucy out. Once she was out and steady on her feet Joe jumped back in with his trowel and started to scrape away round the bag quite vigorously. He stopped and stood up, looked at Lucy, then turned white, or green, I couldn't quite work it out. He held up what looked like a massive femur bone with rotted denim round it and proceeded to scream the entire contents of his lungs out. Lucy hit the floor like a sack of pregnant potatoes and I didn't know what to feel. The secret was about to be out in the open.

Chapter 15 - Blues, Twos and a lot of Commotion

Despite his own screaming chaos, Joe had panicked when he saw Lucy faint, he was also holding a femur and realised that this was a completely unique situation he would never again be in in his entire life. Throwing the bone to the floor, he ran to the car and grabbed the emergency mobile phone and called the police, as if ever there was an emergency, this was it. Thank God for the modern GPRS technology built in phones today, that the police call centre could trace his location, otherwise they would never have been found. In my day I had protested and boycotted phones with such technology, embarrassingly once carrying a sign accusing a local priest of "frazzling babies". All he did was have a mobile phone mast mounted on top of his church as a way to make extra income for the church. It is only now when I am dead do I see the benefit of this technology and how silly I felt now.

By the time the police and ambulance had gotten to the scene Lucy was still sitting on the floor but was awake. The paramedics were great as she was bundled in the back of the ambulance and monitored for a bit to check her labour hadn't started. The police, lots of uniformed and a few of the ones all suited up, it was a sea of black and white swarming round the area. As more units arrived, each van labelled with different text on the side with different jobs of different officers. I knew that this was the day Karl and Katie had their justice. *'Scientific Support'* units were busy with their little boxes and powder brushes, *'Dog Units'* saw the police officers being dragged round by their eager hounds , forensic tents were erected and what looked like aliens in little white paper suits started emerging from the little gap in the tent opening. I was aghast of the whole situation and stood at the side lines just looking at all the hustle and bustle.

I jumped slightly as I heard a young voice behind me say "Bloody hell, look at all this". I genuinely don't know where she came from, but young Katie appeared by my side. I looked at her a little bemused "how did you get here?" I asked, she didn't seem too put out by the whole scene. "I dunno, you know, I was having a sleep in the church and next thing you know I am here". I gathered if Katie was here then not far behind her was Tilly. When she appeared, we exchanged glances before Tilly disapprovingly said "well even though this has happened I told you to leave it be, someone has to look after Katie don't they" she tutted. I reminded Tilly that it was more shocking that she was the church woman, who always insisted that "only God can judge us" was now giving me grief and judging me.

"I found Karl's ghost" I said as a matter of fact to Tilly, "I came here and accomplished what I wanted, all of this, finding their resting place, well this happened by accident". Tilly still unimpressed said quite angrily "So help me God, if I find out you were seen by anyone and directed anyone to here that's me done". Katie rolled her eyes then started dancing off in the direction of the lost soul ghosts further into the woodland.

I couldn't understand where the anger was coming from in Tilly. I would have thought she would've been pleased. I guess she just wasn't buying the serendipitous way it has all happened, or she was annoyed that she was left looking after Katie. I didn't know and to be quite frank I didn't care.

I glanced back at the area and there was Katie looking at a sitting lost soul and I saw that it was my Karl. She was face to face with him and he was looking right through her. You would think that finding his body would have made him snap out of this death beyond death, but he stayed the same. It made me want to weep how he was still lost in this woodland. Tilly and Katie managed to snap me out of my near lost soul experience, and now I was wondering what could I do to make this better.

Chapter 16 - Take us to Church

After the police took all their statements, and the paramedics decided to keep eyes on Lucy for observation, we all hitched a ride from a still shocked, but calmer Joe back to my old house. A police officer drove him in Lucy's hire car, because of Joe's lack of driving licence.

As we approached the town, I suggested that maybe we go into the attic to look at Karl's mirror again to see if it had anything left to show us. Tilly wasn't impressed and looked exhausted but she reluctantly agreed. When we got there as a group of three tired souls, we all looked into the mirror and realised our visit back was in vain as it was just a swirly mess of grey with nothing more to show us. We wandered round the house and then realised that it wasn't just that mirror as all the mirrors had turned into this eddy of clouds that you couldn't see a thing. I found myself starting to wonder what the point of it all was. Their bones had been found and yet they still weren't able to rest in peace. Tilly wanted to go, and she reassured me that she would take care of Katie in the church so I could stay in my old home surrounded by the things I loved.

While there, I stayed under the bed in my old room for days, mainly curled up in a ball. If there were sleeping pills that ghosts could take, I would take them so I could rest in peace artificially. After all the excitement of the last couple of weeks, I couldn't cope with this complete anti-climax. This afterlife was just as unfair as the living life and I didn't want to live here anymore. If there was a way to kill myself in this eternal afterlife then I would.

For weeks I moped around the house watching my granddaughter's bump grow enormous. I saw how after the whole traumatising experience; Joe had certainly had to grow up fast. The neon green paint had turned into an Egyptian cotton paint colour on the walls and the games console room idea had gone out the window.

They were regularly kept up to date with the ongoing investigation and the police visited frequently. It had transpired that Nathaniel had seen the commotion on the news and that night had an unexpected business trip to Spain that needed his urgent attention. What an absolute slimy fucker, he couldn't hide for long. The police investigation saw police officers visiting Lucy and Joe so frequently that they were starting to feel intruded on and like suspects themselves. It wasn't a very calming environment for an already stressed heavily pregnant woman to be in. It also transpired that Nathaniel's wife had also decided to follow him to Spain a couple of weeks later with a one-way ticket and a suitcase of his belongings. With the levels of criminality between them both, it was a wonder how they produced my lovely granddaughter.

As time plodded on, I remained forlorn and hidden and couldn't bring myself to enjoy the arrivals of my great-grandbabies. What was the point, they would never see me or know me alive. I developed my own coping mechanisms and knew that whenever I accidently knocked something over it was time to rest. I cried a lot of the time hoping that Lucy and Joe would go back to Delemere so I could see my Karl again, but I know that experience had scarred them for life. I dreamt about Karl all the time but instead of the soulless zombie, he was chatting as normal talking about all the magical cabaret days and our beautiful daughter Bella. However, he was still so sad and so was I. Sometimes I was sure that Lucy heard my weeping in the night. One-night, I was crying so much that I had scared her. She had reached her thirty fifth week of being pregnant and she was in no position to be getting up listening to me weeping, and being scared. I had to snap out of this.

Even at Lucy's thirty sixth week into pregnancy, the police were still in constant contact with Lucy and Joe. The investigation was very much focused on Nathaniel being the prime suspect for the one who committed these heinous crimes. Lucy was devastated, you could see the reluctance in her eyes about eventually shopping her own father to the police. But what she didn't realise, was that the investigation was at the point that the evidence would have been enough to put her Dad away without any statements. The investigation was still in a heightened state. The fact that there were only bones left, meant an autopsy was harder to perform, needing specialist pathologists and entomologists (a doctor of creepy crawlies and wee beasties to me and you). The police were not able to release her granddad's body to the family, although the other little skeleton, the one of the little girl was released to a family in the same area.

I hadn't seen my companions in a while, however I saw Katie and Tilly on the day Katie's family had decided to bury her remains. Lucy, had done her own research on who the little girl was and her story. She attended the service, but the shame of her DNA made her stand right at the back with her Auntie Bella, who was also up to date with the goings on of her brother. It was the first time since I had known my little spirit friend, that I had seen Katie get upset. She stood by her own coffin at the front of the church and kept touching the polished wood casket. It was a tiny coffin that undertakers would normally put an infant death in, because all that was in there was a brittle pile of bones that her family were laying the rest.

Katie's Mum, Melissa, was absolutely heartbroken. A mother should never have to bury their child as It leaves a pain in your heart that's worse than death itself. My son had denied Katie a dignified burial for which I will eternally suffer the shame, however part of me was happy that Melissa was able to have closure in burying the past, with a truth that she had always known. Her daughter was dead.

Katie stayed in her parents' house that night and openly wept sitting in the corner watching her Mum who was also crying unreservedly. Tilly and I stayed close, but not close enough that either of them could see us or sense us. Even though we had given Katie details on how she had passed, it was time for her to face the actual reality and know how brutal her own death was. I couldn't even imagine explaining death to a child her age who was alive, never mind one that was already dead.

I left Tilly to look after her as I resigned back into my own dark cloud in my own house.

Chapter 17 - New Arrivals

It was in Lucy's thirty eighth week of pregnancy that she went into labour, which was late for someone carrying twins. Doctors had continued to monitor her and reassure her that although her babies had little room to move, that they were doing fine and not creating too many problems for Lucy. Labour started quite suddenly without any induction; she was stood by the washing line pegging out some towels when suddenly she felt like she had wet herself. Reality hit her and she realised it wasn't an accident, and actually it was her waters that went. All the panic and the excitement of the babies suddenly overwhelmed me, which had even surprised me as, I had been so disinterested in my period of second mourning for my Karl's ghost. I wanted to be there in person to see her babies born, I wanted to reassure her that it will all be okay, but this was another way of life that I could never go back to, and the after-life was unfair, I went back to being sad as I couldn't reassure her without scaring her.

Lucy gave birth to two healthy sized babies, one was 5lb 7oz and a little boy, she called Joseph Karl, and a 6lb 2oz little girl who she called Isabelle Katie, because she believed she needed to honour the little girl her father had killed. They were beautiful, so perfect and so healthy. Her Auntie Bella and her cousins were around a lot of the time. This was due to the absence of her own mother and father, still in Spain. But it was comforting to know that in times of crisis we were still a close family. Joe really got stuck in, nappy changing and baby baths and naps were like a military style operation. He gave Lucy enough rest without encroaching on her bonding with her babies. He had gotten so good at cleaning and cooking that I was not convinced it was the same fella who she met all that time ago. I suppose that's what new born twins will do to a man, that or my Lucy had spotted the potential in him when she first met him.

One night when the babies were little more than three weeks old, the house was quiet and the babies were asleep, and then Lucy received the text from her Dad that read "AM HOME, CONGRATS ON BABIES.C U AT 8PM IN URS XX". I panicked, and apparently Lucy shared my panic, I mean what was she meant to do with this information? She knew he was wanted for questioning in her Granddad's death. For the first time since her babies were born, she was tormented. That night, it wasn't the babies that kept her awake, she never slept one wink.

The next morning, Lucy was still troubled to the point that even Joe was concerned. "what's up doll? You are not your usual self". Lucy was dismissive of him, and she did her usual "nothing love, just tired". This went on all day to the point that even I grew bored of her moping, even though I knew why she was moping. It finally stopped when Joe ushered her up the stairs to go to bed for an hour or two.

I didn't think her father could even get into the country again, surely this day in age, with complex international policing, he should have been caught pretty handy. I took this time to go and visit my two companions at out old haunting ground, the church, and I was really beginning to miss their faces.

As I approached the church, I saw Katie running towards me. I was so happy to see a smile on her face. The last time I saw her she was so sad, I mean I don't know what I was expecting her to feel at her own funeral, especially given the circumstances. Tilly was stood behind, still looking as stern as ever, but when I approached with a big smile on my face her defences were instantly disabled and I got a hug. "I've missed you" Tilly said. She had no idea how much I missed her. I hated it when I went into my "waling lady" phases, as I may as well be one of those soulless spirits for all the use I was.

Whether we liked it or not, we had tied up all the loose ends that we needed to, but we were all still stuck together in this form. We had resigned to the fact that this was our life from here to eternity so we may as well get over it.

Tilly had told me that they had visited Katie's Mum again but this time she wasn't very well. Tilly didn't know what was wrong with her, but she herself had to be more careful when visiting. Tilly had been caught once as a "shadow" in the corner, while Katie had terrified her own mother by being that mysterious weight sitting on the bed. The kind of things that you only hear in ghost stories.

I told them about the babies and the joy that was in the old house. I had no choice but to tell them about Nathaniel's upcoming visit. "What are you going to do?" asked Tilly. "me?, listen Til, you are always telling me off for getting my nose stuck in where it's not belonging in the living world, why change your mind?" Tilly looked a bit sheepish, caught out in her own logic, "I don't know, it's not right really is it?" I was getting a little frustrated with her now. "what can I do exactly?" I asked hypothetically. Without realising it was a hypothetical question Tilly had one word. "Justice".

We started out the walk back to Lucy's home as a trio.

When we got there Lucy was awake from her nap and Joe was in the kitchen making tea. The babies were both lying in their own little Moses baskets. Katie went right up to her little name sake and started cooing at her.

Something didn't feel right about the scene in the old house. It felt artificial, staged and tense, however it was business as usual and Joe and Lucy were getting along well, there were no signs of a previous row. Lucy was pulling on the sleeves of her own jumper looking nervous. If she didn't stop pacing up and down, the carpet would be thread bare. She kept pacing to the mirror and looking at herself and I noticed there was a fear in her eyes. Joe came out the kitchen with a bowl of salad and placed it on the dining table. "It will be okay doll, don't worry about it". They both heard the car park up outside their house and Lucy whispered to herself "its show time". I looked out the window and saw it was Nathaniel and his wife.

Lucy's mum was looking rather tanned. She looked completely out of place in the suburban street, with her gaudy costume jewellery, white jacket and pink floral print parachute pants. She had two gift bags on her arm as she teetered up the path in her high heels shoes that looked rather too small for her swollen feet. Nathaniel looked older than he did before he went on the run. Any brown hair he had left had turned into grey. With his overly dark tan he was far from the "silver fox" look he was going for he looked more like Santa Claus, who had holidayed in Hawaii.

Lucy opened the door but blocked the way, so as to not let them cross the threshold, "how dare you show up knowing what you have done?"

"Darling", her Mum piped up "I don't know what you are talking about, but your Dad's investments have a habit of failing, sometimes an extended holiday can help shift some of the bad people away, but I want to see my grandbabies, it isn't a crime is it?" She barged past Lucy into the house. Lucy stood in her Father's way before he could enter and whispered through gritted teeth, "you haven't told her have you, you murderer". He smiled back at her, got right up to her face and scowled, "and she's not going to know is she, or you and your dickhead husband will be joining Karl, darling". Every consonant of the word Darling was pronounced and the venom apparent in his voice. "I am warning you now, do NOT deny your mother her grandchildren, you little witch"

With his venomous outburst, me Tilly and Katie were absolutely livid. Katie looked at him with a kind of mixed hatred, "was it him?" she asked, with an eerie calmness. Tilly didn't even know what was happening, she was outraged and blind with her own rage. "I am going to take Katie outside" she doesn't need to see him, but Katie tried to insist she stay "I don't want to go, please don't make me go". "Listen Katie", I said "there's nothing we can do here, so its best if you wait outside with Tilly". She gave me a reassuring nod and walked out the door.

The tense feelings continued as I watched Lucy's Mum hold the little girl. "Oh darling, she's beautiful". Lucy went to the chair and picked up her little boy and then sat down with him. Nathaniel was a different person in the presence of cooing babies, than the one who had only ten minutes ago threatened his own child. "so Lucy bear" Nathaniel enquired "what have you called the little miracles". When Lucy told him the names, Nathaniel's expression dropped. "You vile little witch" he retorted. Lucy's Mum was aghast with shock, "What the hell is wrong with you Nathaniel?" Joe stood up and his usual weak stance disappeared. "I am asking you to leave, please do not talk to my future wife like that".

Nathaniel looked like he was about to launch Joe across the room, but instead he stood nose to nose with him, snarled and said "Come on love, we are leaving, I knew this was a bad idea". Lucy's Mum gently put the baby back in her Moses basket and said "no Nathaniel I am going to stay here for a while, you should leave now and come back for me later".

Nathaniel was livid, but conscious of there being babies in the room, so he just turned around and walk towards the door. When he reached for the handle he was stopped by a knock. "were you expecting anyone?" he asked a little shocked. "Might be" Lucy said smugly. He calmly put the handle down and it was a man in a suit. Nathaniel was never a stupid boy, he had just made some bad decisions, so he knew what this situation was straight away, there was one man, and down the path was a police car with a uniformed officer stood at the door of his vehicle, and I couldn't help wondering if this the end of the road for him.

What I never saw, was that while Lucy was having her "nap" she had been in touch with the police in order to tell them about her father's return.

"Mr Nathaniel Lange, is it, do you mind stepping back in so I can talk to you"

Nathaniel shoulder barged past the man and towards his car. "no sorry, I am busy, move". In his car I could see Tilly and Katie in the back seat so I ran to join them.

"Sir, I am asking you to stop" insisted the suited man as Nathaniel got in his car and turned the engine. The suited man ran towards to police car and told the other officer to get in and drive

I got in Nathaniel's car just in time for him to speed off. The police car was in hot pursuit. It was an odd sort of excitement we were all feeling, but still scary as Katie was snuggled tight into Tilly. "Why did you get in his car" I was trying to ask while going all over the place in the car. "Tilly said "I don't know, we just did, we wanted to see if there was any more proof here. "YOU'RE DEAD" I reminded them, "what were you going to do with it once you found it!"

The chase had begun. He hit the motorway and turned off at a quiet junction to get into more country roads. We heard the whirling blades of the police helicopter above, as more cars had joined the pursuit. Katie and Tilly were actually scared but I don't know what for, they couldn't exactly die again could they! Regardless of the irony of the two already dead people being scared of dying, something had to stop this. The living people that were wondering on the pavements, could be the next dead spirit people in this car. I don't want to see any more victims of my son's reckless driving, because my son's killing count was already two more than what it should be already.

Katie scrambled over us in the back and climbed in the front passenger seat. She sat and closed her eyes and gave out the almightiest scream. It was a scream that sounded like a million demons were talking through her little mouth. Nathaniel turned his head and took his eyes off the road for one second and saw that little girl in front of him. She turned and looked him direct and carried on screaming like a banshee. Tilly was covering her ears and balled up on the back seat. Nathaniel looked in to rear view mirror and I knew he saw my face, with my eyes turned white and my mouth also joining in on the screaming.

I don't know what compelled me to do it but I was just as loud with more demonic screams added to the mix.

There was an obvious wet patch in Nathaniel's lap as he started screaming as well, but in his case, out of pure fear. It seemed like it was taking an age, but in real time it was a second. In that split second, he took his eye off the road, the car hit a curb and turned over into a sign post and into a hedgerow that was protected by a small wall.

For some reason our ghostly bodies weren't tossed around by the car. Without actually willing it to happen we all disappeared from the inside of the car including the balled-up Tilly, then we suddenly reappeared all upright and stood by the wreck. Nathaniel's almost lifeless body was lying there with a piece of the car's metal chassis, twisted into a point, starting to penetrate his chest, above his heart.

I hovered above my child with a tear in my eye, but an anger that couldn't be tempered. I started to lean on the twisted metal and looked my son in the face. "I know you can see me son, I've not come to get you, because they don't let people like you stay on this earth". The concentration I had as I started to push the piece of twisted metal further into his heart and kept pressing it until he gave his last breath.

I watched Nathaniel's spirit come up from the car wreck. I stood back, then I saw him run towards me and pushed my spirit away from him. "WHAT HAVE YOU DONE?" His spirit was about twenty years old, the same age he was when he killed young Katie Hoyland. He was so absolutely angry, he showed no remorse, no shock at realising he was dead, no shock that he was looking at his dead mother. Something strange happened, small spiders started coming up from the ground onto him. He flicked a few of the little critters off in his rage, and then when they started coming rather thick and fast, he looked down and panicked. He started shouting angrily, "get them off me, help me Mum". My boy needed me, but I froze. What could I do? It was like my feet were planted into the ground; I could only watch him panic. I started to choke on my tears as I watched my baby boy scream and cry, as millions of little spiders enveloped him like a walking black mass. Then like a magician's cloak the spiders dropped to the floor and Nathaniel was gone.

I turned around, still sobbing from witnessing my child disappear, back to the car, to see the police cars pulling up. They couldn't see us three by the side of the road but we could hear them. "Jesus, if he survived that I will be surprised" one officer said as he radioed in that he would need ambulance and fire engine support.

The chatter of the policeman and the incoming sirens had just turned to one mass of noise. None of it concerned me, so the noise started to fade. I closed my eyes, still wet from tears, but this time, when I opened them, I was in Delemere forest. Katie and Tilly were no longer with me. That's when I saw him. I saw my Karl. He wasn't the zombie version we had seen in this misty forest before, but a gorgeous ghostly version of the living Karl.

"Hello my beautiful Isabelle" he said. I cried as I ran up to him and held him so close. It had been so long since I had seen him. "now now Isabelle, it's done now. Thank you".

When we hugged each other, we began to glow. I was wondering, was this when we go to our Other Place, or could be stay on here and watch my family grow up. I knew that young Katie's Grandma had come back from the Other Place, so I knew it was possible for fleeting visits.

I looked up at my Karl and still couldn't believe that I had him back. I can't believe he was so calm. He spoke so softly, "what's wrong Izzy?" he asked.

I couldn't take me eyes of him. "Is this it? Is this where we go? I have waited so long to see you again and now have to go off into nowhere"

"Oh, but Isabelle, I've spent so long trying to be one of the living, just to find out what happened to the girl that Nathaniel killed, that I was lost myself. Let's not kid ourselves shall we, let the living live, and now I have you back, lets enjoy it together in peace"

I smiled at him, and he smiled back. This was why I loved him so completely. He was the only one who ever managed to talk any sense into me.

We glowed until the light shone so bright there was nothing there anymore.

We went to our Other Place.

Afterwards

My Name is Katie Hoyland

When Isabelle disappeared, Tilly stood there in shock. "Well Katie, I'm sorry but I think I am going to have to go, I was only here to look after Isabelle". I looked at her a little confused.

"Why are you still here then?" I asked her

"I don't know, if I am honest, let's get you back to somewhere that you know", Tilly said.

Nathaniel's car had taken us so far out of the way, that I had no clue where we were, or how we were going to get back. We waited around in a police car that the suited policeman came in, in the hope that he would be going back to break the news about Lucy's Dad. Me and Tilly got in the back of the car and rested. It was harder to rest with all the hustle and bustle of the police lights, and metal on metal crunching as the bust-up car was put onto a flatbed lorry

A couple of hours later, the suited police man and his friend, the one who had a police uniform on, got in the car and started to drive back towards the town. He stayed silent for most of the journey with only the little hisses off his radio interrupting the silence. It was about twenty minutes into the journey that he said to his mate, "do you want to tell her or should I? I don't envy the head fuck that's going to happen after this"

Tilly rolled her eyes, she hated everyone swearing. They stopped at Izzy's old house and we got out. But just as we had put our feet on the pavement, Tilly disappeared.

I had been here on my own before, so I thought I'd be fine without my babysitters now. I mean, I am oldest out of them, I mean that I've been deader longer than the both of them.

Tilly and Isabelle probably forgot, that even though I was still a kid when I died, I don't get to see what I would grow up to look like as an adult. Izzy could be thirty-eight as she had been thirty-eight before. I had only ever been ten. I still knew better than them both, how to do more in the afterlife then them. But yet here I am, I don't know why I'm still here and yet they figured out how they move on.

I ran as fast as my legs could take me, direct to my Mums' house. As I walked through the door and went up the stairs, my brother, sister and my Mums grandchildren, were all sitting or walking around my Mum's house, pacing the carpet until it was bare.

She was really sick now, and I could see that it wouldn't be long before I was holding her hand and seeing her again, but this time in my world.

Kate, my niece, was asleep on the camp bed at the end of Mum's bed. It was supposed to be her turn to keep an eye out as her Mum, my lovely sister, was putting the kettle on.

I sat on her bed and my Mum looked right at me. She could see me. My Mum said in gasp and with a laboured breath, "Hello Katie doll, I knew you would come". A tear ran down her face. "Hello Mum, I've missed you", as I tried to touch my Mums tear with my see-through hands. I don't want to see my Mum crying; she was and always will be my Mum.

I held her hand, and my Mum's transparent hand came out of her body and began grasping mine. I lifted her spirit from her broken vessel while her family, also my family, gently slept nearby. She stood up from her broke body and looked down at herself. She smiled and her last breath escaped the body.

She was young again. She was the Mum I knew. She hugged me "oh Katie doll, I failed you, I loved you, I am sorry".

"I love you Mum"

We went to our Other Place.

The End

Printed in Great Britain
by Amazon

32063431R00076